A 365 Day Guide to Becoming a Bride

Venicia Lloyd

from various sources. Please consult a licensed professional before attempting any techniques outlined in this book.

By reading this document, the reader agrees that under no circumstances is the author responsible for any losses, direct or indirect, that are incurred as a result of the use of the information contained within this document, including, but not limited to, errors, omissions, or inaccuracies.

Table of Contents

Introduction

'I've known him for 13 years. We're childhood sweethearts. I can't imagine my life with anyone else. But sometimes, I wonder if he feels the same about me. I don't know what to do anymore!' said Natalia. 'I met someone. He seems perfect. But how do I know if he's the one God has planned for me? How do I know it will work out this time? What if I end up getting hurt again?' asked Sarina. 'I sometimes worry that I'm growing old. No one will want an old woman as their wife. I might never be able to have kids then', expressed an anxious Doreen. 'Trust in the Lord, girls! God loves you, and He hears you. He will lead you to the right man at the right time', the Women's Life Group leader at their local church encouraged them.

Maybe you're someone who is in a situation similar to these women. You probably desire to get 'married' but you're unsure about the man you're dating. Maybe you're hoping that your partner will change for the better after marriage. Or perhaps, you have questions about God's standard for relationships and marriage. Maybe you've been praying for the right man to come along, but the season of waiting often makes you anxious. Perhaps you struggle with feelings of rejection and trauma from your past relationships or experiences. The fear of being rejected or hurt again is stopping you from moving on in life. Maybe you've struggled with commitment in the past. Or maybe you feel like you can't love enough—two years is the longest you can keep the relationship going. You probably struggle with understanding your partner, which leads to many unreasonable fights in the relationship.

While our anxious thoughts and feelings about marriage may weigh us down, we have the one who is ever faithful—He, the unchanging and everlasting God. The Bible in Philippians Chapter 4 tells us to be anxious about nothing but give thanks and pray about everything. And the peace of God will guard our hearts and minds. In 1 Peter Chapter 5, the Bible tells us to cast all our burdens on Jesus because He cares for us. God is faithful. His plans and ways are above ours. We often fail to understand His plans for our lives, but we must trust Him. God is our loving Father, and He has good things in store for us.

Through this book, I trust that you will know and understand the purpose of God for your life and marriage. You will learn to seek the Lord to find your spouse. As you read through this book, you will understand your calling as a woman of God. You will learn ways to prepare your hearts and minds for marriage. You will know the standard that God calls you to as a wife. You will also learn about God's plan for your relationship and marriage. As you read through this book, you will learn about love as God intended it to be.

You will learn about the power of effective communication. This book also talks about dating without compromising on God's standard for our lives.

It talks about honouring God in our singleness and togetherness. You will understand the needs of men and how God designed them to be unique. This book talks about the feelings and emotions of men. You will also learn about governmental order in the family according to the Bible.

Through the course of this book, trust the Holy Spirit to minister to you. This book is a step-by-step guide to becoming a bride. It will walk you through the difficulties that women often face when choosing their spouses. It will answer the questions you may have on dating and marriage. I pray that you will grow in your intimacy and relationship with God and your spouse and glorify our Father in heaven. Read on to know what it takes to become a bride to the man of your dreams.

Chapter 1:

Be Intentional

Did you ever, as a little girl, dream about your wedding day? You have probably imagined yourself all dolled-up in a white gown walking down the aisle to the man of your dreams. As women, almost all of us have thought of our big day. And most of us have had our entire wedding day planned out before we even knew who we were going to marry. Some of us have even thought of and planned the little details of our wedding day—the perfect dress and hairdo, fresh flowers and pretty lights, bridesmaids, the venue, and maybe even the hymns. When we were younger, many of us may have played dress-up with our girlfriends or may have even pretended to marry our primary school crush. On average, a woman starts planning her wedding day at the age of 13. Some girls begin planning their wedding as early as the age of 5 or 6.

I think it has something to do with how our Creator God has beautifully designed us to be. We are God's masterpiece. We have been fearfully and wonderfully made by Him.

Then God said, "Let us make mankind in our image, in our likeness"' (Genesis 1:26 NIV).

'Then the Lord God formed a man from the dust of the ground and breathed into his nostrils the breath of life, and the man became a living being' (Genesis 2:7 NIV).

'The Lord God said, "It is not good for the man to be alone. I will make a helper who is just right for him"' (Genesis 2:18 NLT).

'So the LORD God caused the man to fall into a deep sleep; and while the man slept, the LORD God took out one of the man's ribs and closed up the opening. Then the LORD God made a woman from the rib, and he brought her to the man' (Genesis 2:21-22 NLT).

'"At last!" the man exclaimed. "This one is bone from my bone, and flesh from my flesh! She will be called a woman because she was taken from a man. This explains why a man leaves his father and mother and is joined to his wife, and the two are united into one. Now the man and his wife were both naked, but they felt no shame' (Genesis 2:23-25 NLT).

'You made all the delicate, inner parts of my body and knit me together in my mother's womb. Thank you for making me so wonderfully complex! Your workmanship is marvellous—how well I know it' (Psalm 139: 13-14 NLT).

'For we are God's masterpiece. He has created us anew in Christ Jesus, so we can do the good things he planned for us long ago' (Ephesians 2:10 NLT).

God designed us to be relational. The most intimate relationship that a man and woman can share is in marriage. We were created one for the other—woman for man. It is in our very nature to want to relate intimately with the opposite sex. It is no wonder then that we begin planning our wedding at such a tender age.

As little girls, we are unable to fully comprehend the concept of marriage. We are drawn more towards the flowers, pretty lights, and the romance it entails. Our fathers are the first male figures in our lives, often our superheroes. If we have been blessed with good fathers, we often imagine our future husbands to be just like our fathers. Finding the right man through the eyes of an innocent little girl may have seemed like a breeze. However, as you grow older, you begin to see more of the world. You begin to meet more people—some are good to you and perhaps the rest are not as kind. You probably dated a couple of guys who did not end well for you. Now that you are ready to get married, you suddenly realise that finding the right man is probably one of the biggest decisions you might have to make. It does not seem as simple anymore.

How do I know when I have found the right one? How do I know this is from God? Is he the one for me? These are common questions that women often ask when seeking out their life partners.

Women put so much time and effort into planning the perfect wedding day that we forget to plan and prepare for the institution of marriage. What do I mean by that? The wedding day is just 24 hours of your life. The real deal begins from the 25th hour onwards 'till death do us part'. Yet, we spend a major part of our lives planning for the mere 24 hours rather than for the rest of our lives. We plan the specifics of our wedding and know exactly how we want the wedding day to be. But how many of us have thought of and know exactly the kind of man we want to be with?

Every girl wants a handsome hunk, but that is not what I am talking about. You will be spending every day with this man for the better part of your life. Have you thought of how he might react and handle difficult situations? Have you thought about the kind of father he will be to your children? Will he be able to lead your family well as the spiritual head of the house? Remember that marriage is for life. God holds the marriage covenant as sacred. God's standard for marriage is high, and divorce is not an option. So, it is important to choose the right man. But how is that possible, you might ask? Well, it's certainly not impossible with the God we serve. Our God is alive, He is a prayer-answering God. We can go to Him about anything, as He is faithful and well- able to give us what we ask for in His name.

'Where there is no vision, the people perish; but he that keepeth the law, happy is he' (Proverbs 29:18 KJV).

As you read this chapter, I hope and pray that you will learn to pinpoint exactly what you desire in your future partner.

Let's Be Really Specific

Marriage in itself is hard work. Good marriages don't just happen. It takes prayer and effort to make a good marriage. But a godly spouse can make a big difference. Finding the right man can make your marriage beautiful and exciting. When we were younger, many of us wrote down a list of things that we wanted in our future husbands. If you're one among them, now is a good time to look for that list. If you've never had a list before, I encourage you to prayerfully identify and write down a few things that you desire in your future husband.

It may seem like a silly thing to do, but God our Father already knows what is on your heart, and He is interested in every little detail of your life. It's not silly to Him. He wants you to approach Him like you would with your earthly father. As kids, we asked our dads for anything we wanted, no matter how silly we thought it to be. Put forth your requests to God in the same way. He hears your prayers and will give you your heart's desires. God desires to give good gifts to His children.

'Take delight in the LORD, and he will give you your heart's desires. Commit everything you do to the LORD. Trust him, and he will help you' (Psalms 37:4-5 NLT).

'Which of you, if your son asks for bread, will give him a stone? Or if he asks for a fish, will give him a snake? If you, then, though you are evil, know how to give good gifts to your children, how much more will your Father in heaven give good gifts to those who ask him!' (Matthew 7:9-11 NIV).

Jade, a friend of mine who recently got married, was born into a Christian home. As a little girl, she attended the local church service regularly with her parents. She narrated how her Sunday school teacher would teach the kids in the class to pray for their future spouses. The teacher had taught the girls to pray about the kind of man they wanted. She also taught them to pray for protection over their future husbands. And they prayed that God would prepare their hearts for marriage whenever the time was right for them to meet. Jade prayed this prayer every day for 21 years until, at 27, she met James, the answer to her prayers. She married him and continues to pray for him every day.

Be specific with what you want in your future husband, even if it is something as simple as an activity that you really enjoy doing. Make specific requests to God about it. True, God already knows what is on your heart, but He wants you to ask Him for it and trust Him. He wants you to grow in your relationship with Him as you trust in His plans for your life. Throughout the Bible, we see stories of how people made specific requests to God and He was faithful in answering them.

God was faithful to Hannah. He answered her prayers by opening her womb and blessing her with children (1 Samuel 1). The Lord answered the prayers of Abraham's servant sent to find a wife for Isaac *(Genesis 24)*.

'Keep on asking, and you will receive what you ask for' *(Matthew 7:7 NLT)*.

Persevere in prayer with faith. Believe that God is well-able to give you what you desire. God is the same prayer-answering faithful One, and He will surely hear your specific requests about what you desire in your man. So, be confident when praying about it. Put your faith into action and don't be afraid to be very specific.

A close friend of mine, Jessica, loves dancing. When Jessica knew she was ready to get married, she wrote down a list of things that she desired in her future husband and began to pray the list through. 'A man who loves to dance' was one of the many things Jessica listed as a priority. When she met Jason, she knew he was the one God had in store for her. He was everything she had prayed for and more. And yes, you guessed it right, Jason loves to dance! Jessica is grateful to God for the man in her life. She is all the more grateful whenever he asks her for a dance.

The Bible doesn't give us an extensive list of instructions to follow while choosing a spouse. God allows us the freedom to choose the person we want to marry; however, there is just one instruction that is mentioned in the Bible:

'Do not be unequally yoked together with unbelievers' (2 Corinthians 6:14 NKJV).

The Bible is very clear about God's will for us in choosing the right man—he has to be a follower of Christ. There is no compromise here. It's the most important characteristic to desire in your future husband. It isn't because we're a bunch of narrow-minded religious fanatics, but rather we are children who love and serve the Most High God. Our ultimate purpose is to glorify God and prepare ourselves for the return of Jesus, and the right man will do just that for you. A good Christian man will share the same values as you in Christ. The right man won't hold you back but will always lead you closer to God. He will uplift you in prayer when times get tough and help you grow in your relationship with the Father. A Christian husband will follow the lead of the Holy Spirit. He will lead the family well as the spiritual head of the house.

He will strive to love you like Christ loves the church—with sacrificial love. Christ loved us, His church, so much that He gave up His life so we could live. It is the standard of love that God requires of a husband. And only someone who has experienced this sacrificial love of the Saviour will be able to give of himself to love you in this way.

'Husbands, love your wives, just as Christ also loved the church and gave Himself for her' (Ephesians 5:25 NKJV).

Many argue that you can still have a good marriage after marrying an unbelieving husband. While it might be true, you are surely going to miss out on God's intended idea for marriage in all its fullness. You are also most likely going to lose out on the purpose of your marriage. The wrong partner can draw you away from worshipping God and cause you to worship other gods and idols.

Look Out for Red Flags

'He used to be such a sweetheart. I don't know what has gotten into him ever since the wedding day'. 'He's changed. He's not the same man I married'. 'He doesn't respect my parents or me anymore'. 'He won't attend the church service with me'. 'He won't even pray with me anymore'.

Too often, unfortunately, I've had wives tell me that their husbands have changed a few months or even years into the marriage. But the chances are that the men they married were always that way. Their wives simply failed to notice it before marriage—they were blinded by love. Love is blind until we get married, and then the blindfolds fall off. Don't walk into a marriage blinded by love. It can lead to a downward spiral that may be disastrous to your marriage. Instead, seek the counsel of the Lord and save yourself a great deal of pain and heartache. God has intended marriage to be a beautiful union of two souls and bodies. Your husband should never be your cross to bear.

We live in a time where social media and the Internet play a big role in our lives. We are constantly exposed to worldly standards of love, romance, and relationships. The ways of the world are slowly creeping into the Church and Christian marriages. These worldviews distort the standard that God has intended for us. We need to guard our hearts and lives against these corrupt ways that are not only dangerous to us but also rob God of His glory. God instructs us not to conform to the patterns of the world. He calls us to be a holy people. He calls us to be continually transformed by the renewing of our minds.

'Don't copy the behaviour and customs of this world, but let God transform you into a new person by changing the way you think. Then you will learn to know God's will for you, which is good and pleasing and perfect' (Romans 12:2 NLT).

'Guard your heart above all else, for it determines the course of your life' (Proverbs 4:23 NLT).

We can be easily influenced by what we watch. Our eyes are a doorway to our minds and hearts. Be cautious about what you subject yourself to. Keep your eyes fixed on God and on things that are eternal. Live your life according to the Word of God, not according to the recent rom-com that you watched. The Bible says that the human heart is untrustworthy above all things. So, it is unwise to make a decision based only on your feelings. You need to be guided by the Holy Spirit in everything you do, including choosing your partner. Ask God for wisdom when it comes to choosing the right man.

'If any of you lacks wisdom, let him ask of God, who gives to all liberally and without reproach, and it will be given to him' (James 1:5 NKJV).

God has also given us common sense. Often, the red flags are right in our faces—do not ignore them! Many times, we marry someone with the hope that they will change after marriage. However, it is very unlikely. And if they don't change, you're still stuck with them. Changing a man's heart is the work of God and the Holy Spirit. Don't flirt to convert. Don't marry a man to change him, as I assure you that you will be disappointed.

It is wise to get into marriage with the full knowledge of the man you will be spending the rest of your life with. Understand his shortcomings and weaknesses. Remember, however, that no man is perfect. It all comes down to what you're willing to overlook to grow together in your journey as man and wife. At least you'll know what you're getting into and what's worth fighting for.

It is easy to identify red flags when you ask the Holy Spirit to remove the blindfolds of love from your eyes.

'Yes, just as you can identify a tree by its fruit, so you can identify people by their actions' (Matthew 7:20 NLT).

'But the Holy Spirit produces this kind of fruit in our lives: love, joy, peace, patience, kindness, goodness, faithfulness, gentleness, and self-control' (Galatians 5:22-23 NLT).

You can tell a Christian by their actions and the fruit they bear. It is natural for people to feel different emotions, even anger. What's important is how they react to these emotions. What kind of fruit does he bear? Is he patient and loving during disagreements or does he lose his temper and resort to violence? Many times, people tend to blame their reactions on their situations. But we know from the Bible that our thoughts, words, and reactions flow from what is deep within our hearts.

'A good person produces good things from the treasury of a good heart, and an evil person produces evil things from the treasury of an evil heart' (Luke 6:45 NLT).

Think of the heart like a sponge. When you squeeze a sponge, it releases what it has soaked up. In the same way, when a man is 'squeezed' in any situation, he will release what he has been soaking up. If he has been feeding himself with the Word of God, he may get angry or upset but will show self-control and be quick to forgive. No one is perfect. And yes, there are a few times when they may slip and let their emotions have the better of them. But does it happen once in a while, or is it a repetitive pattern that you've noticed? Look for patterns.

You will also know the kind of man he is by the relationship he shares with his parents. How does he treat and talk about his parents? Is he grateful and respectful towards them or does he resent them? God instructs us to honour our parents whether they have been good to us or not. If a man cannot honour and respect his parents, he is never going to honour and respect you. Perhaps he holds the door open for you, but would he do the same for his mother? If the answer is no, then chances are that he is putting up a front for you, and it's not going to last very long. Be wise and discern between a man trying his best to change and a man who is set in his ways.

Since you met him, do you feel like your relationships with God and the people around have improved? What are his priorities? Is he passionate about his Saviour? Does he have a relationship with God? Does he pray and read his Bible? He should be committed to a local church where he grows and receives regular edification. Is he eager to serve? Did he serve in his local church before he met you? I've known men who have served at a Sunday service only to impress the girl they were dating. This is a big red flag. Our servanthood should come as a response to God's love for us and our obedience to His Word. We should be able to serve even when no one is watching. A man who serves well only in public will struggle to serve you and your marriage well in private behind closed doors. We learn to serve selflessly by following Jesus' example, and our lives should bear testimony to it.

Every marriage has its ups and downs. When you're in a fight, the last thing you want is for your husband to hold something against you forever. Is he quick to forgive? Does he have a grudge against you or anyone else? God forgives us and doesn't hold our sins or our past against us. A good Christian man will do the same for you.

Another red flag is forcing you to submit to his authority. Submission should come as a natural response to his leading and love for you. It should come from a place of understanding and recognising his ability to lead you and the family. Forced submission is like being bound in chains in prison, where your partner is in control of everything. It is an unhealthy relationship and is not how God designed the marriage union.

The company he keeps when he isn't around you is also an indication of his character. Who are his close friends? Does he share good friendships with other believers? It is important to have unbelieving friends who we can influence for the sake of the kingdom. But we need to be careful not to be swayed by their ways of life and stand firm in our faith.

Another red flag is forcefully trying to make the relationship work. When a relationship is from God, you will notice that things begin to fall into place naturally and beautifully. If you have to second-guess the person on several occasions, you might want to take some time out to pray and be sure about it. I'm not talking about pre-wedding jitters here. I mean the absence of peace or a feeling of uneasiness in your heart.

A close friend of mine met a Christian man at a Christian Leaders Conference. They really 'hit it off' and soon began dating. Even though he was a believer, there were several red flags around him that she chose to overlook. She hoped that he would change with time. Within a year of dating, he proposed. They got engaged and began planning their wedding. The strange thing about it though was that every time they set a date for the wedding, they were required to postpone it due to unforeseen circumstances. This pattern went on for almost a year. She says that at one point in time it felt like they were forcing the wedding to happen. So they took some time out to pray about it, and that's when she realised that she felt no peace about it anymore.

Sometimes, when we have made up our minds about a man, we tend to align our thoughts and feelings to believe it is from God without actually seeking His counsel. Thankfully for my friend, the Holy Spirit removed her blindfolds of love just in time, and the wedding was called off.

Maybe you're in a relationship, but you haven't had peace about it for a while now. Take it to the Lord in prayer. It could be a nudge from the Holy Spirit. We need to understand that God loves us and wants to give us what is best for us, even though we often don't see it that way. God sees the big picture; He sees our entire lives. We need to learn to trust His plans and ways for our lives.

'For my thoughts are not your thoughts, neither are your ways my ways, declares the LORD. As the heavens are higher than the earth, so are my ways higher than your ways and my thoughts than your thoughts' (Isaiah 55:8-9 NIV).

Break free from a toxic relationship. Seek help from your spiritual leaders if you need to and save yourself from a lifetime of abuse and torture. If you're wondering how you're going to handle the heartbreak, God assures you that His grace is sufficient for you. Have faith and trust in Him.

'My grace is sufficient for you, for my power is made perfect in weakness' (2 Corinthians 12:9 NIV).

Set Personal Boundaries

It is healthy to set personal boundaries early on in the relationship. Talk about your boundaries with your partner and let him know how you feel. Boundaries are not to simply enforce right and wrong but are a means of protecting yourself and your partner. If you do not end up marrying the one you're dating, remember that tomorrow he will be someone else's husband. Boundaries function as barriers against temptations that will cause us to stray from God. Boundaries will help us prioritise God's way above our own ways and desires and will ultimately help us honour and glorify the name of our Lord.

Spiritual Boundaries

Setting spiritual boundaries include not compromising on your Christian values for anyone or under any circumstances. It is better to honour God in your singleness than to be in an unwise marriage. Let your partner know what you stand for in Christ and that you are unwilling to compromise on any standard mentioned in the Bible. Let them know that you will build your relationship on the truth, with Christ as the foundation. Set boundaries to honour God in everything that you do, especially when no one is watching.

Physical Boundaries

Setting physical boundaries is very important. Physical affection is a common way in which we express our love. Physical touch in itself isn't wrong, but it opens the doorways to sexual temptation—it is what will eventually lead you there if you let your guard down. How far is too far? The Bible is very clear on sex before marriage—it is a big NO! Prayerfully decide what is too much for you before you get into a relationship and lay out your boundaries when you start dating. What are you comfortable with? Perhaps you can agree on hugs and holding hands. Let him know that he needs to ask if it's anything outside of what you decide is okay. Maybe you can agree to hang out with a group of friends or in a public space. You can also agree not to meet physically after a particular time in the evening or avoid meeting in secluded and dark places. Quite contrary to what the world tells us, don't cross boundaries that shouldn't be crossed. Live your life according to the Bible.

Relational Boundaries

We were created to share a good relationship with God and our spouse. We were also created to share a good relationship with other people around us. When we start dating, we often want to spend all our time with our partners. It is natural for both to feel that way. However, we need to value our existing relationships with other people too. While your relationship with your heavenly Father is the most important, don't isolate yourself from other close relationships when you start dating. Yes, your relationship with God is the foundation for all other relationships in your life. But you will need other people to be a part of your lives as individuals and as a couple.

Don't ditch your girlfriends when you think you have found your man—they are often the first ones who can notice and will point out potential red flags in him. Keep your spiritual mentors and leaders in the loop about your relationship. It will help you to stay accountable. They will pull you back on track should you stray from the Lord's ways. Set clear boundaries when it comes to relationships. Sometimes, you might have to let him know that as much as you would have loved to, you can't hang out because you already have plans with your family or friends. Setting relational boundaries could also mean letting him know that Sundays are reserved for church services.

Emotional Boundaries

Setting emotional boundaries will help you manage your thoughts and feelings. We must take responsibility for our actions. Often, we tend to assume that our partner knows what we are thinking or what we want. Men can't read minds any more than women can. Express how you feel. Let him know what is on your mind. Be direct about it and avoid manipulation. Avoid blaming him for situations, especially when you're upset. Do not indulge in name-calling. The Bible exhorts us not to let any unwholesome talk come out of our mouths. Sometimes, you may need to tell him that you need a few minutes to gather your thoughts and compose yourself so you can speak respectfully.

When it comes to setting boundaries, prayerfully seek the leading of the Holy Spirit. Set boundaries for yourself before you get into a relationship. It'll be easier to stick by them when you are in a relationship.

Self-Care: Confidence vs. Rejection

As you seek the Lord and pray about your future husband, it is equally important that you also prepare your heart for marriage. Take a moment to reflect and discern why you want to get married. Knowing why you want to get married is as important, if not more important than knowing what you desire in your future husband. What is your mindset? Are you getting married to fill the void you feel in your heart? Maybe you think that marriage will make you feel less lonely? Maybe for some, age is a pressure. You want to get married because you feel like your biological clock is running out of time. Are you getting married because all your peers are married and you feel left out at get-togethers? Or perhaps, you are looking to feel loved and happy and you hope that marrying a good man will do the trick for you. These feelings arise from a place of insecurity or rejection.

Rejection is the lack of unconditional love and acceptance. 'Rejection often leads to the fear of rejection'. Let me try and explain that. Maybe you were in a relationship with a guy. You thought he was the one; everything was going great. But then he dumped you for another girl. Or perhaps you found out that your partner had been cheating on you. You felt rejected. You probably felt like you weren't good enough. These feelings of rejection from past relationships can stop you from moving into what God has planned for you. Maybe you like someone now but your past experiences keep reminding you that you were rejected before. Who's to say that you won't be rejected again? You probably think that this relationship will never work because you don't believe you will ever be good enough for him. These thoughts are the fruit of rejection. They arise when we do not fully understand who we are in Christ.

When we struggle with our identity in Christ, we tend to put very little worth or value on our lives. We think that we don't deserve the best and are okay with settling for the second-best. We begin to believe that this is what we deserve because of our experiences and sins in the past. You probably think that it is God's way of 'punishing' you for your past ways. But these are the lies of the enemy. The Bible tells us that the wrath of God was poured out on Jesus on the cross. Jesus was punished in our place for our sin, so we never have to be. He was killed so we can live. We can have life because of Jesus' sacrifice on the cross for us. When you repent of your sin and put your faith in Jesus, His righteousness wipes you clean.

'For God did not appoint us to suffer wrath but to receive salvation through our Lord Jesus Christ' (1 Thessalonians 5:9 NIV).

'And since we have been made right in God's sight by the blood of Christ, He will certainly save us from God's condemnation' (Romans 5:9 NLT).

It is true that without God, we are nothing. But when you accept Jesus as your Lord and Saviour, He gives you a new identity. You are no longer a product of your past because you are now a product of the cross. You become a child of the Most High God; you are a new creation in Christ; you are royalty.

'This means that anyone who belongs to Christ has become a new person. The old life is gone; a new life has begun!' (2 Corinthians 5:17 NLT).

'But to all who believed Him and accepted Him, He gave the right to become children of God. They are reborn—not with a physical birth resulting from human passion or plan, but a birth that comes from God' (John 1:11-12 NLT).

'For you are a chosen people. You are royal priests, a holy nation, God's very own possession' (1 Peter 2:9 NLT).

The Bible tells us that God gives good gifts to His children. God wants to bless us. He wants good things for us, and He knows what is best for us. We need to start seeing through the eyes of faith and believing the truths of the Bible for our lives.

'Every good and perfect gift is from above, coming down from the Father of the heavenly lights' (James 1:17 NIV).

Remember, thoughts of condemnation are not from God but from the enemy. Jesus sent the Holy Spirit to the earth as He ascended into heaven. The Holy Spirit is our helper and guide. He often points out areas in our lives that need correction and a refreshing from God. As we grow in our relationship with God, we will become more sensitive to the leading of the Holy Spirit. The Holy Spirit brings conviction in a way that is loving and causes you to repent. On the other hand, thoughts of condemnation are from the devil.

'But the advocate, the Holy Spirit, whom the Father will send in my name, will teach you all things and will remind you of everything I have said to you' (John 14:26 NIV).

We need to know our identity. We need to know who we are in Christ. When we are motivated by anything else other than our relationship and intimacy with Jesus, we often end up making unwise decisions. Don't choose to settle for the second-best when you can have the best that God has in store for you. Don't just rush into marriage to escape from your insecurities. Instead, face them head-on by the power of the Spirit and the finished work on the cross.

You must deal with your baggage before you enter into a relationship and marriage. Don't enter marriage to be fixed or to fix someone else. Be transformed by God first and then get into a relationship. You can't turn to a man or your spouse to make you happy; your happiness should come from God alone. Your husband or partner is like a bonus—he should simply add to your happiness. He shouldn't be the sole source of it in your life. He can't fill that void in your heart—it can only be filled by Jesus. You are complete in Jesus and not through marriage.

Think of your heart as a jigsaw puzzle with one missing piece in the shape of a cross. No other piece will fit that empty space. No other relationship, or money, or education, or any other pieces will fill that empty space. We often try to find the missing piece in other things in our lives. But the puzzle will never be completed with any other piece except the cross. We will always feel a void in our hearts unless we allow the cross to complete it. Jesus is the missing piece and nothing else will make us feel complete.

As you wait for your future husband, allow the Holy Spirit to work in you. Don't just waste your singlehood, instead use this time to grow in your relationship with the Father. Marriage is a responsibility; it is for life. This is how God intended it to be. It requires unending effort and commitment on your part. If you think you are not ready for that level of commitment, then you are probably not ready for marriage yet. It is better to wait and honour God in your singleness than to be in a marriage that dishonours God. The Bible also teaches us that some people may be called to a life of singleness. The Apostle Paul speaks of it as a gift.

'But I wish everyone were single, just as I am. Yet each person has a special gift from God, of one kind or another' (1 Corinthians 7:7 NLT).

My pastor always tells the young adults in his congregation this: Don't get married to be happy. Get married to make the other person happy. Often we look at what we can get from a relationship, rather than what we can give to it. When our partner or spouse can't meet our needs and expectations, we are disappointed. Many couples decide to call it quits when they feel like they can't get anything more from their relationship. It is no wonder that so many relationships fail and marriages end in divorce, including Christian marriages. It is estimated that 50% of first marriages will end in divorce.

The Bible teaches us that it is better to give than to receive. However, we cannot give what we do not have. Remember that our joy should first come from Jesus. Only then will we be able to serve others out of the abundance of joy that God puts in our hearts. As you begin to give more of yourself in marriage, you will be blessed with the ability to give and love all the more.

'You should remember the words of the Lord Jesus: "It is more blessed to give than to receive"' (Acts 20:35 NLT).

'If you are faithful in little things, you will be faithful in large ones' (Luke 16:10 NLT).

As you and your partner begin to serve each other sacrificially, you find that your relationship will start to blossom and bear more fruit. It will set the foundations for a good marriage.

God's Standard for a Woman

The Bible sets the standard for a godly woman in the book of Proverbs 31. It talks about a wife of noble character. As you read this passage of scripture, ask the Holy Spirit to minister into areas of your life that need to change:

10 'A wife of noble character who can find?

She is worth far more than rubies.

11 Her husband has full confidence in her

and lacks nothing of value.

12 She brings him good, not harm,

all the days of her life.

13 She selects wool and flax

and works with eager hands.

14 She is like the merchant ships,

bringing her food from afar.

15 She gets up while it is still night;

she provides food for her family

and portions for her female servants.

16 She considers a field and buys it;

out of her earnings she plants a vineyard.

17 She sets about her work vigorously;

her arms are strong for her tasks.

18 She sees that her trading is profitable,

and her lamp does not go out at night.

19 In her hand she holds the distaff

and grasps the spindle with her fingers.

20 She opens her arms to the poor

and extends her hands to the needy.

21 When it snows, she has no fear for her household;

for all of them are clothed in scarlet.

22 She makes coverings for her bed;

she is clothed in fine linen and purple.

23 Her husband is respected at the city gate,

where he takes his seat among the elders of the land.

24 She makes linen garments and sells them,

and supplies the merchants with sashes.

25 She is clothed with strength and dignity;

she can laugh at the days to come.

26 She speaks with wisdom,

and faithful instruction is on her tongue.

27 She watches over the affairs of her household

and does not eat the bread of idleness.

28 Her children arise and call her blessed;

her husband also, and he praises her:

29 "Many women do noble things,

but you surpass them all".

30 Charm is deceptive, and beauty is fleeting;

but a woman who fears the Lord is to be praised.

31 Honour her for all that her hands have done,

and let her works bring her praise at the city gate' (Proverbs 31:10-31 NIV).

Through the book of Proverbs 31, God is calling on us as women to be compassionate, joyful, kind, selfless, and loyal. He calls on us to be women of faith, wisdom, justice, and self-control. God wants us to be good friends and neighbours to the people around us. He calls us to be hardworking and lead fruitful lives. He also calls on us to be secure and strong women, deriving our strength from knowing our identity in Christ. God calls us to be mothers and good stewards of what He has given us. You may not have children of your own, but you can be a spiritual mother to someone. And most importantly, God is calling us to be women who love the Lord and fear Him.

This may seem like a long list of things for you to get right. You may fail at some or all of them, but you must try and never stop trying. It is not possible to live a holy life according to God's standard by our own strength. We need to rely on the Holy Spirit for help. We can be confident that God never fails us.

Overcoming Past Trauma and Rejection

Do you know who you are in Christ? Do you know that you are loved and accepted by Him? Or do you struggle with thoughts and feelings of rejection?

Perhaps you have been hurt by your friends time and again. Or maybe you find it hard to trust people. You don't have too many friends and have trouble keeping the ones you have. Maybe, you were in a relationship that didn't end well for you. Or perhaps you watched your parents go through an ugly divorce when you were a child. Events like these can make us feel insecure and are often the root causes of rejection.

Many times, our experiences can be traumatic and can leave a deep wound on our hearts. Maybe you had an abusive father. Or perhaps, you were hurt by a previous boyfriend or a male figure you looked up to. You want to get married, but you can't get yourself to trust anyone again, let alone a man. You may even wonder if you will ever be able to love again as you have in the past. Our present feelings and fears usually stem from deep roots of rejection. But there is hope for you. God wants to heal your heart and make it whole again. The Bible tells us that God reaches out to the broken-hearted. He wants to fill your heart with His love so you will be able to love again.

'The LORD is close to the broken-hearted and saves those who are crushed in spirit' (Psalm 34:18 NIV).

'He heals the broken-hearted and binds up their wounds' (Psalm 147:3 NIV).

'And this hope will not lead to disappointment. For we know how dearly God loves us, because he has given us the Holy Spirit to fill our hearts with his love' (Romans 5:5 NLT).

The first step to dealing with past trauma and rejection is acknowledging that you need help. You can't do it in your own strength and need the grace of the Father. You need the Saviour. Jesus died on the cross so you can live free from the bondage of your past. He was rejected, so you can be accepted. Understanding God's original plan for mankind is important in dealing with and overcoming feelings of rejection. God created man and placed them in the Garden of Eden. We were made to live in an atmosphere of unconditional love and acceptance under the covering of the Triune God. He designed man to have a sense of security and belonging. Our need for identity, love, and acceptance were all provided for by God in the Garden of Eden. But then man sinned and was separated from God. We have since been yearning to satisfy our need for identity, love, and acceptance. Restoring our relationship with the Father is the key to dealing with issues of rejection.

Be real about your past. Don't try to deny or hide the pain that you feel. Acknowledge that the rejection you've faced has affected your behaviour and life. People who feel a lack of acceptance are often insecure people. They try to cover up their insecurities by behaving in ways that may exhibit their strengths. Many people who face rejection often show emotions of anger. They can be controlling, people-pleasing, judgemental, and critical. Our sense of security comes from God alone. He is our defence.

When we place our security in anything else, we are allowing it to take the place of God in our lives. The Bible says that this is sin—nothing should take His place. Reflect on your life and recognise if you show any of these behaviours. Ask the Holy Spirit to show you patterns in your life that are sinful and may have arisen from rejection. Take responsibility for your behaviour and repent. Healing will happen as you recognise and release the pain. Release forgiveness towards people who have not treated you well. Forgive yourself for your wrong decisions and mistakes in the past. If you struggle with forgiveness, talk to your spiritual mentor or a leader in your church whom you can trust. They will pray with you and help you walk out victorious.

Remember that your past doesn't define you but Jesus does. Continue to choose to walk in victory as you live in total love and acceptance, knowing that you are secure in God.

Chapter 2:

What's Love Got to Do with It?

Love is the foundation of all relationships.

God exists as a Trinity as God the Father, God the Son, and God the Holy Spirit. This identity of God can be explained simply as three beings or persons in one nature of God. All three persons exist in a perfectly harmonious relationship with each other. This explains why God is love. It is a marvellous mystery that our finite minds cannot fully comprehend. The Trinity of God reveals His very nature of being loving. The very essence of God is love.

C. S. Lewis in his book, *Mere Christianity* (1952), writes: 'The fact that God is loving requires that God is relational. The fact that God is relational requires that He is loving. If God is Triune, you know He is love. Because you can't have three people existing in perfect harmony without being loving'.

The Bible shows us how God ideates the meaning of love through His character. Right from the time of creation, to the fall of mankind, and to the plan of salvation, God is our perfect example of love. When

God made man in His image, He imparted this very essence of being 'loving' into man. He put in man the longing desire for intimate relationships. However, since the fall of mankind, sin has distorted mankind's idea of what true love is.

When man disobeyed God and sinned, he was separated from Him. It wasn't because God didn't love him anymore, but rather because He is a holy God and sin has no place around Him. Our sin makes us feel distant from God. God never stopped loving man. His love for us is unconditional and unfailing—He loved us even when we were undeserving of it. God demonstrated His love for us by sending His only begotten Son to die for us on the cross. Jesus' sacrifice for us is the perfect example of love.

'But God demonstrates his own love for us in this: While we were still sinners, Christ died for us' (Romans 5:8 NIV).

'For this is how God loved the world: He gave his one and only Son, so that everyone who believes in him will not perish but have eternal life' (John 3:16 NLT).

Understanding God's love for us is vital to our lives. It is the key to all the other relationships we share. Our relationship and love for God will determine how we relate to and love people around us, especially our spouse. We can only give love if we have first experienced it ourselves. They say hurting people hurts others. But according to the standard that God has set for us, I'll say that loved people love others. If we have not experienced the love of God in our lives, we will find it hard to show love to people around us. It is the sacrifice of Jesus on the cross that has enabled our relationship with the Father to be restored. It is because of the love that we experience through Jesus that we can genuinely love those around us. This genuine love we share will help us enjoy an intimate relationship with our spouse.

Dear friends, let us continue to love one another, for love comes from God. Anyone who loves is a child of God and knows God. But anyone who does not love does not know God, for God is love. God showed how much he loved us by sending his one and only Son into the world so that we might have eternal life through him. This is real love—not that we loved God, but that he loved us and sent his Son as a sacrifice to take away our sins' (1 John 4:7-9 NLT).

'We love each other because He first loved us' (1 John 4:19 NLT).

God, through the Bible, really stresses the importance of love. The greatest command given to us is to love the Lord with all our hearts and minds. This isn't because God needs our love or is incomplete without it. Instead, it is because He knows that it is hard for us to build a strong foundation outside of His loving guidance. It is hard for love, peace, blessing, and prosperity to exist in any area of our life but for the loving guidance of our heavenly Father. Our love for our partner or spouse should flow from the love that we have for God. Does your partner love God more than he loves you?

Jesus replied, "You must love the LORD your God with all your heart, all your soul, and all your mind'. This is the first and greatest commandment. A second is equally important: 'Love your neighbour as yourself" (Matthew 22:37-39 NLT).

The other equally important commandment that Jesus gives us is to love our neighbours as ourselves. Most of us don't have trouble loving ourselves. Some of us might be a little too much in love with ourselves. While the world tells us that self-love is the most important, God is calling us to a higher standard of love. God calls us to love our neighbours. He doesn't stop there, but goes on to say that we need to love them as we love and take care of ourselves. This is not to say that God disapproves of self-love. His standards are just higher— He calls us to find self-love in Him through Jesus.

The Bible teaches us that there is no greater love than the man who lays down his life for his friend. Jesus demonstrated this greatest form of love when he laid down His life for us. We need to live and love by the example that Jesus set for us. This doesn't mean literally killing yourself to show your partner that you love him. Rather, it means sacrificing our own needs and desires for the one we love. It means putting them before us. God calls us to love even when the other person is undeserving of it. In everything that we do, with the help of the Holy Spirit, we should become more like Jesus. When we love our partner or spouse, especially when it's hard to, our lives will reflect Jesus. It depicts His sacrificial love for us when we were still sinners. According to God's standard, our love should be sacrificial love or self-sacrificing love. This is quite contrary to what the world teaches us about self-love.

'There is no greater love than to lay down one's life for one's friends' (John 15:13 NLT).

What Is Love?

Couples who split often say that they 'fell out of love' or don't 'feel' like they love their partner or spouse anymore. But love is more than just a feeling. Love is a conscious decision that you make every day. It is a choice to love, especially on days when it is hard to love. It is easy to love someone in the good times. The real challenge is in loving someone when things go bad. According to the world's standard, you may continue to love your spouse as long as there is a mutual 'feeling' of affection or attraction. When reciprocity is broken, the 'feeling' of love begins to die. The marriage also dies along with it. Many couples believe that once the usefulness of their relationship is done, it is time to move on. However, this is not God's standard of love and marriage for us. The biblical concept of love is unlike that of the world. It is more intimate, more sacrificial, more demanding, more generous, and more giving than receiving.

If you love only those who love you, why should you get credit for that? Even sinners love those who love them!' (Luke 6:32 NLT).

The pastor at the church that I attended always said: 'Choose the one you want to love and then love the one you choose'. Choose the one you want to marry and then commit to loving him in the good times and the bad times. It is not always easy to love unconditionally. At times when we struggle to love, we need to look to the cross for strength. The grace of God is sufficient to sustain us in the hard times. We need to depend on the Holy Spirit. We need to constantly grow in our love for God so we can express what is in our hearts. Experiencing the love of God in our lives is not a one-time event. We need to experience it in our lives daily. Everything we do, including loving our partners, should stem from the intimacy and love we have for God. Only then will we be able to love to our full potential, according to the standard that God has set for us.

Through His life, Jesus shows us that true love is self-sacrificial. It is generous and not self-seeking or greedy. True love is unending; it is not a temporary 'feeling'. It is also undeserving and unconditional.

The Bible clearly lays out God's standard of love for us. You can use the following scriptures to measure the love you give to people in your life. You may also use it as a measure for your partner or spouse.

4 Love is patient and kind. Love is not jealous or boastful or proud or rude.

5 It does not demand its own way. It is not irritable, and it keeps no record of being wronged.

6 It does not rejoice about injustice but rejoices whenever the truth wins out.

7 Love never gives up, never loses faith, is always hopeful, and endures through every circumstance' (1 Corinthians 13:4-7 NLT).

It is not possible to obey these lofty commands in our flesh. Many of us fail at just the first one—love is patient. We cannot fulfil the standard of love that God calls us to in our own strength and willpower. We need the grace of God and the power of the Spirit to reach there. We will be able to love better as the Lord gives us the strength to do so.

What Does Being Loved Feel Like?

Many a time, people turn to other means and forms of love to fill the void in their hearts. They go from one relationship to another in the hope of finding a sense of fulfilment or completeness. But this often leaves them feeling worse and incomplete. One way to tell if your partner is acting out of the love that he has experienced is to observe how freely he gives. Love is not just a mere declaration of your love to the other person. The Bible talks about loving through our actions and deeds. It is proof of our love. We see the perfect example of this love demonstrated by Jesus on the cross. God loves us so much that He 'gave' His Son for us even when we didn't deserve it. True love is a 'giving' love. Loving someone comes from a place of being loved by God. It comes from a place of being complete in God.

'Dear children, let us not love with words or speech but with actions and in truth' (1 John 3:18' NIV).

Is your partner a giving person? How is he towards people who have hurt him in the past? Has he forgiven them? Does he pray for them and bless them, or does he still hold their wrongs against them?

We often act out our love from the love that we have received and experienced. You feel loved when you understand the work of the cross. As you reflect on Jesus' sacrifice on the cross, you will begin to realise how you didn't deserve to be loved and forgiven. Yet, God saw it befitting to love and forgive sinners like us through His Son. He not only forgives our sins but also remembers them no more. The knowledge of this truth makes it easier for us to love and forgive people who have hurt us. The more love we receive from God, the more we will want to give. God doesn't love us because we are good but because He is good. We have freely received this love from God. We need to give as freely as we have received.

The Bible also teaches us that the Lord disciplines those He loves. A man who loves you will want to see you grow to become more like Jesus. He should be able to respectfully disagree with you and point out areas in your life that need correction. He shouldn't simply agree with everything you say to keep you happy but rather bring correction to you in love.

'For the LORD corrects those he loves, just as a father corrects a child in whom he delights' (Proverbs 3:12 NLT).

Being loved also makes you feel secure in knowing that you are loved dearly by the God of the universe. The truth that nothing can separate you from the love of

God makes you confident in knowing that God wants to give you the best. It helps you trust in His plans for your life. There is a sense of joy and contentment that comes from knowing that God loves you. This is the joy that you should experience and have in your heart before you decide to get into a relationship. Make sure your partner also shares the same joy in the Lord as you do. Together you will be able to rejoice in the Lord!

The Importance of Communication

Communication is essential for every relationship to function. It is the key to knowing and understanding what is on one's heart. As we express our thoughts and feelings to our partners, we are communicating with them. Some people, especially men, may struggle with effective communication. They may find it hard to express and communicate how they feel. Men often feel like they need to put up a brave front at all times. This idea may have originated from the values of society. Be patient with your partner. Allow him to feel comfortable enough to talk about what is on his heart and mind. Be respectful towards him. Avoid belittling or mocking his ways and thoughts.

Men cannot read minds. Most men don't get the subtle hints that women give them. They like to be direct and expect the same from their partner. Don't just assume that they know what you're thinking or how you feel. You must communicate your thoughts and feelings to them. We often assume that men know or are supposed to know what we are upset about. But more than often, most men are clueless that their partners are even upset. Talk things through. Communication develops a better understanding in a relationship when it is real and heartfelt. Go beyond just words. Share your feelings and emotions with your partner or spouse. Don't try to bottle up how you feel and instead be real with him. Another important aspect of communication is handling conflicts and disagreements. Don't push things under the rug. Sort out and settle the conflict before you go to bed. The goal should be the resolution of the conflict rather than trying to prove oneself right.

State your opinion. If it's something you like or dislike, communicate it to your partner. He will appreciate it. Many times, people tend to take offence when we point out ungodly patterns or behaviours in them. However, be expressive about what you think even if you feel that your partner might not like it. If it is done with good intentions and in love, your partner will eventually see it. Although initially his ego may be tickled, he will see your heart behind it and even appreciate you for telling him. You need to allow him to do the same for you. However, how you say what you want to say is important. Don't be rude or harsh with your words. Be gentle in your tone while communicating with him. When something sensitive has to be addressed or communicated, be led by the Holy Spirit about how to do it. Approach it in prayer. Do not leave God out of the equation.

The more open you are with each other, the better the communication will be. Avoid keeping secrets from your partner. Don't give the devil a foothold in your relationship. Build your relationship on the foundation of truth and trust. Talk about what you expect from the relationship. Make sure that the two of you want the same thing from the relationship, whether it is marriage in the future or kids. You need to be at a place in your relationship where you are completely free with each other, to be honest about everything. Ask the tough questions at the beginning of the relationship. When you ask difficult questions and have difficult conversations, you have nothing to lose. Instead, you will get to know each other better. We may fear that our partner will judge us because of our past. But if you have repented of your sins, God has forgiven you. He has washed you clean and remembers your sin no more. There is no shame and no guilt anymore. Don't let the devil condemn you. Know that you are loved by God. It is unfair to your partner to have to know things about you from someone else. Before you enter into marriage, make sure there are no skeletons in the closet. Be led by the Holy Spirit about when and how to share things about your life with your partner.

How your partner reacts to what you share with him will tell you how your relationship will span out in the long run. Does he taunt you or condemn you? Does he gossip about it? Or does he pray for you and encourage you? God doesn't hold your sins against you and neither should your partner.

Set the building blocks of communication early on in your relationship. One way to let the other person know that you care about what is happening in their lives is to ask them about their day. Avoid talking in clichés. Make sure that you are only communicating facts and not stories from your imagination. It is important to also share ideas and judgements. You may not always share the same thoughts and ideas, but you can choose to respectfully disagree with your partner's opinions.

When it comes to setting personal boundaries, especially in your courting days, talk with your partner about what you think is okay. Men are wired to be problem-solvers. They often feel like it is their duty to fix things. That is why when you tell your partner about a problem that you are facing, his first response is to give you advice on how to resolve it. However, women often simply want a listening ear—we may already know the solution to the problem we are facing. We often communicate to de-stress. We need to communicate this to our partners. Let him know that while you appreciate his heart to fix things for you, at the moment, you want him to simply listen to you without giving you advice.

It is important to communicate effectively. Many times, what we say and what our partner hears and perceives can be very different. This may lead to misunderstandings between the two of you. You can communicate with your partner by making eye contact and showing interest when he talks to you. Make sure you understand what is being said by inquiring with questions. Set aside your phone and other external distractions to help you give all your attention to your partner. Communicate that you would like him to do the same for you. Pay attention to his body language so that you understand the emotion behind his words.

Communication is a two-way line. When one speaks, the other one listens. Both cannot be speaking at the same time. Women often complain that their partners don't listen well enough to them. But we must admit that we women also love to talk. We have to take time and learn to listen to what our partner has to say. We need to learn to listen as attentively to his work stories as we would expect him to listen to ours. Many of us may not be good listeners. But fortunately for us, listening is something that can be learned. We can grow in our listening skills as we also practice listening to God. Sometimes, our prayer time is like a one-way communication with God. We're always telling Him what we need or how we feel. But how often do we take the time to listen to what God is speaking to us? As we listen to God and improve our communication with Him, we will also improve it with people around us.

Communication will connect your hearts before marriage. Be careful about what you communicate. It should always build you up and not put you down. The Bible tells us to be careful about our speech. Talk to your partner exactly how you would like to be spoken to, especially when you're upset. When you talk to others about your partner, speak true and good things about him. It will help you value him better. Speaking ill of him shows disrespect towards him and can cloud your view of him. The right form of communication will ensure you feel respected, validated, and understood.

'Don't use foul or abusive language. Let everything you say be good and helpful, so that your words will be an encouragement to those who hear them' (Ephesians 4:29 NLT).

Communication in Love—The Five Love Languages

Learning your partner's language of love is as important as learning the language of the country you live in. We need to understand and speak the emotion of love. Gary Chapman in his book, *The Five Love Languages,* brilliantly explains the different kinds of love languages. He writes that there are mainly five languages of love that people speak. What your partner or spouse often requests of you is most likely to be his love language. The way we express our love to our partner or spouse indicates our love language. Communicating and understanding the love language of each other will help us love more effectively.

Words of Affirmation

Words of affirmation include verbal compliments. Learn to compliment and appreciate your partner for who he is. Express your love to him verbally. Let him know how much you mean to him. Words of affirmation are kind and encouraging. They are also humble requests and not ultimatums. Love makes requests, not demands. You can write down positive things about your partner that you can say to him at a later time. Affirm and praise him in front of others when he is around. Say positive things about him when he is not around.

'Kind words are like honey-sweet to the soul and healthy for the body' (Proverbs 16:24 NLT).

Quality Time

Many people love through the language of quality time. We can get so busy with our routines and work that our interaction with our partner or spouse may be limited to a phone call. Taking time off your usual routine to be with your partner will help you strengthen and refresh the relationship. Quality time doesn't mean simply going on a date. It involves giving each other undivided and focused attention. Spending quality time with your partner shows him that you care about him and that he matters to you above everything else. It indicates to him that you enjoy his company; you enjoy making him the centre of your attention. It brings in a feeling of togetherness in the relationship.

When you spend quality time with your partner, make conversation and refuse to be interrupted. Put your phone aside and disconnect from your work. It is your time with your partner. For some, spending quality time together might mean going on a date and enjoying a good meal together. For others, it could mean doing a fun activity together like painting or trekking. For still others, it may be as simple as watching the sunset together. It doesn't matter what activity you do, make sure you are at the centre of each other's attention.

Receiving Gifts

Gifts are considered to be a visual expression of love. Giving gifts is the best investment you can make in a partner or spouse whose love language is receiving gifts. Note down the things that your partner or spouse has expressed excitement about receiving. You don't have to wait for a special occasion to gift him something. If you are a person who saves and budgets everything, you might find some trouble with the idea of spending money as an expression of love. But if it means making your partner feel loved, do it anyway. However, don't buy things you can't afford just to impress your partner. The heart of love is in the spirit of giving. Give cheerfully. Your physical presence is sometimes the best gift that you can give to your spouse.

Acts of Service

Acts of service involve doing things for your partner that you know he would like you to do. These acts make him feel loved. Maybe you can take his car for a wash. Or maybe, make him a cup of coffee in the morning. Acts of service involve loving in actions and deeds and not just through words. It is one thing to tell your partner that you love him and a completely different thing to express that love to him through your actions. Acts of service require thought and planning.

They also require time, effort, and energy on your part. Always look to Jesus as an example of selfless service.

Physical Touch

Physical touch doesn't only mean sex. It is a powerful communicator of love. It also involves embracing your partner or spouse and holding hands. It includes cuddling with your spouse and expressing your love to him physically. However, while you date, make sure to set physical boundaries to keep yourself from dishonouring God.

The Benefits of Friendship Without Titles

When you meet someone, take your time in getting to know him. Aim to have a healthy friendship with him. Grow your friendship and let it take its course. Don't be eager to give your relationship a title even though you may have feelings for each other. Giving your relationship a title brings in expectations. Instead, get to know him as a friend.

The world has a different viewpoint on relationships without titles. It tells us that two people who get into an unlabelled relationship, do so because they don't want to commit. The world today uses terms like 'friends with benefits' and 'non-exclusive' to define their 'untitled' relationships. But this is not what I mean. I'm talking about a healthy and God-centric friendship. It is a friendship that builds you up and encourages you to become a better version of yourself.

'As iron sharpens iron, so a friend sharpens a friend' (Proverbs 27:17 NLT).

You can hang out with a mutual group of friends. It gives you time to get to know the other person better. It is easier for him to put on a front when he is with you alone. But when you hang out in a group, you can observe how he treats and reacts with other people around. People tend to be themselves when they are around other people who you're comfortable with. Not giving your friendship a title will also allow you to set boundaries and stick to them. You will know if you share similar values and common interests. As good friends, you can do things together that you enjoy or be willing to participate in activities that one of you enjoys doing. You can also try out new activities together.

Don't try to rush things. In due time, you will realise that he is your best friend and the one who supports you. He has probably seen the worst but has stuck by you through it all. He has also perhaps already met your family. You like how he loves and gets along with them. You will also be confident in knowing that your family adores him. As you realise that he loves you, you will naturally grow in your relationship together without having to give it a title. If the Lord wills it, you will end up marrying your best friend.

Sheila met her husband, Levi, when she was 19. She was still studying and moved to a university in a different city a few months after she met him. She mentions how her mother encouraged her to pursue the friendship she had with Levi, without giving it a title. She advised Sheila to finish college and see how she felt about it. They hung out in a group of mutual friends whenever she was back home. Sheila says it was the wisest thing to do because it gave her time to really pray and think about Levi as her potential husband. The time they spent away made them realise and understand why they wanted to get married to each other.

Uncorrected Conduct Becomes Repeated Conduct

Relationships, including marriages, often fall out due to misunderstandings that arise from a lack of communication. When issues are swept under the rug and not dealt with at the earliest, they tend to pile up. When we do not address the conflicts we face with our partner, we tend to pile up emotion over emotion. Until one day when we can pile up no more and finally let our feelings explode. This is almost never a pleasant sight for the person on the receiving end, often our partner or spouse.

God created us as emotional beings; we were created to emote. Emotions are a healthy part of our human nature. We are called to express how we feel through our emotions. We may express emotions of sorrow, joy, and even anger. These are God-given ways to deal with situations and circumstances in our lives. But often the expression of emotions is perceived as a sign of weakness. So we tend to suppress and bottle up our emotions and feelings. Some people at the other end of the spectrum may resort to harmful and dangerous ways of expressing their emotions.

Often, our pride and ego get in the way of addressing issues and resolving conflicts. Pride often unnecessarily escalates minor issues and situations, causing them to blow out of proportion. 'It was his fault. He should apologise first!' 'She always blames me for everything when it's really her fault. I always apologise first. Let her apologise first this time!' These are common thoughts that go through our minds when we are in conflict with our partner or spouse. Don't let pride get the better of your relationship. You need to lay your pride at the foot of the cross. You need to come to a point of humility in Christ and address the issues or undercurrents in the relationship. Everyone makes mistakes. You lose absolutely nothing by apologising first, even if it isn't your fault.

Often, we blame our partners for the way we react. 'He provoked me. He made me react this way'. 'He made me so angry that I couldn't control the way I reacted'. Stop blaming your partner and take responsibility for your own actions. Sometimes it's true that our partners do provoke us, but the choice to react in a certain way still lies with us. No one can force you to react in the way that you do. You are designed to control your emotions and not the other way round. Yes, we can struggle with our emotions, but with the help of the

Holy Spirit, we have no excuse for our impulsive reactions. The Bible teaches us not to sin in our anger.

'And "don't sin by letting anger control you". Don't let the sun go down while you are still angry, for anger gives a foothold to the devil' (Ephesians 4:26-27 NLT).

'Be angry, and do not sin. Meditate within your heart on your bed, and be still' (Psalms 4:4 NKJV).

Deal with today's issues and conflicts today. Put them to sleep as you go to bed. Do not bring them up again just like how you cannot bring back the day gone by. Disagreements and conflicts in a relationship are normal. But fight so that you never have to fight about the same thing again. This should be the goal of your conflicts. It is a healthy way to deal with the problem. Remember that your partner is only human. He will make mistakes, as will you. Be quick to forgive just as your Father in heaven is quick to forgive you.

Chapter 3:

Butterflies

'You'll know he's the right one for you when you feel the butterflies in your stomach as you kiss. 'I know he's the one for me because he makes me weak in my knees'. Maybe you have said things like these or have heard people say them.

You can feel your heart racing every time he looks and smiles at you. You can't help but blush when you steal a glance at each other during the church service. Your heart skips a beat every time you hear him tell you that he loves you. You feel an electric warmth flow through your body every time you hold hands or hug. No one else makes you feel the way that he does—he gives you butterflies in your stomach! You can't wait for your next date because you love the butterflies. He makes you feel all mushy, and you love it! While butterflies in your stomach are great, they can also lead you down the wrong path if you let your guard down.

Perhaps you're someone who has never felt butterflies in your stomach, and you're probably wondering if he's the right guy for you. You're probably waiting to feel the butterflies so you can decide if you want to marry him or not. Because if he can't make you feel this way now, it'll only get worse in marriage, right? Not quite.

People generally get strong feelings of butterflies in their stomachs in the initial years of dating. But what happens when, after a few years, you don't feel them anymore? Does it mean you are out of love? The butterflies that you feel in your stomach are but a natural reaction that takes place in your body in response to certain situations. They make you 'feel' good. But feelings can be deceptive, and butterflies can lie. They are not a sign that he is the one for you, any more than him turning up for the date is. You always need to seek the counsel of the Lord whether you feel butterflies or not.

Love is more than just feeling the butterflies in your stomach. It goes much deeper than just surface feelings. We need to act according to the guidance of the Holy Spirit and not how we feel because the Bible tells us that our hearts are deceitful. Your relationship and marriage should be based on Christ's standard of love and not on your feelings. Instead of butterflies, look for the peace of God within your hearts. Trust God and not the butterflies.

'The human heart is the most deceitful of all things' (Jeremiah 17:9 NLT).

'Trust in the Lord with all your heart; do not depend on your own understanding. Seek his will in all you do, and he will show you which path to take' (Proverbs 3:5-6 NLT).

Our beliefs about love and romance are, to a large extent, influenced by what we watch, hear, and read. Some novels and movies are based on love stories. Sometimes they depict intricate details about sexual intimacy, while at other times they paint a very rosy picture about feelings. While these are great means of entertainment, they may very subtly distort our ideas about love and relationships. We may begin to govern our relationships according to the standards of the recent rom-com movie we might have watched. However, as Christians, we need to live according to the standard that God has set for us. A relationship built on the solid foundation of Christ's love will stay strong and endure testing times.

47 'As for everyone who comes to me and hears my words and puts them into practice, I will show you what they are like.

48 They are like a man building a house, who dug down deep and laid the foundation on rock. When a flood came, the torrent struck that house but could not shake it, because it was well built.

49 But the one who hears my words and does not put them into practice is like a man who built his house on the ground without a foundation. The moment the torrent struck that house, it collapsed and its destruction was complete' (Luke 6:47-49 NIV).

You and your partner need to practice the fruit of self-control in your relationship while dating. There are a ton of fun things that you can do together and sex isn't one of them. Yes, sex is great but only when it is enjoyed within the bonds of marriage. It is the most intimate relationship that a man and woman can share. God designed this intimacy to be shared only in marriage. The Bible warns strictly against sex before marriage. While butterflies make you feel mushy and warm, don't get carried away by them.

'A person without self-control is like a city with broken-down walls' (Proverbs 25:28 NLT).

Physical affection is a way to express our love for our partner, but it also opens us to sexual temptation and sin. We might think we have it under control. But one thing leads to another, and often we don't realise we have fallen prey to sexual temptation until long after. The Bible tells us to literally flee from sexual temptation and sin.

'Run from sexual sin! No other sin so clearly affects the body as this one does. For sexual immorality is a sin against your own body' (1 Corinthians 6:18 NLT).

We see a classic example of this from the life of Joseph, who fled from Potiphar's wife when she tried to seduce him.

7 'After a while his master's wife took notice of Joseph and said, "Come to bed with me!"'

8 But he refused'... (Genesis 39: 7-8 NIV).

10 'And though she spoke with Joseph day after day, he refused to go to bed with her or even be with her.

11 One day he went into the house to attend to his duties, and none of the household servants was inside.

12 She caught him by his cloak and said, "Come to bed with me!" But he left his cloak in her hand and ran out of the house' (Genesis 39: 10-12 NIV).

Be careful if your man is too eager to get physical too soon in the relationship—it is a red flag. Set boundaries and stick to them. However, since we are human, we fall. Boundaries may be crossed—everyone slips. But this shouldn't be used as an excuse to compromise on the laws set out for us in the Bible. Try to discern the intention behind it. Was it an accident or intentional? Ask the Holy Spirit for strength and help to stay away from temptation.

Everything we do revolves around the physical as well as the spiritual realm. It is wise not to get in too deep too quickly when you start dating—relationships are not merely physical. The spiritual element of the relationship is called a 'soul-tie'. Soul-ties aren't formed only through sexual interactions. They also form when you connect intimately on an emotional level. The Bible uses words like yoke, bondage, knit, joined or cleave, and bound up to express soul-ties. These relationship-ties greatly influence our lives. It is not about the person but rather what we do with that person that can form an ungodly soul-tie.

A good way to distinguish a godly soul-tie from an ungodly one is by discerning the spiritual hold over the relationship. A godly relationship and soul-tie is a union based on love. There is freedom, edification, and blessings over the relationship as God intended it to be. Ungodly relationships are governed by fear and bondage. Ungodly soul-ties are about exhibiting control. Soul-ties need to be broken before we enter into marriage. Talk to your spiritual mentor or leader about your previous relationships that may have resulted in the formation of ungodly soul-ties. Especially deal with soul-ties that may have formed from multiple sexual partners in the past. Ask them to pray with you and break the soul-ties. There is mercy, forgiveness, and love at the foot of the cross. There is freedom in the name of Jesus.

Often when we have set our minds on something, we have very little trouble finding an answer to the questions that we might have. We try to look for advice and answers that justify our actions or desires. We tend to stick to the advice that confirms what we wanted to do in the first place without checking it with the Word of God. We hear what we want to hear, and it doesn't matter who is offering the advice. But the Bible teaches us that while everything is permissible, not everything is good for us. Make sure we feed on the Word of God and get our advice from it. We should always be led by the Spirit, even in our relationships.

12 'You say, "I am allowed to do anything"—but not everything is good for you. And even though I am allowed to do anything, "I must not become a slave to anything".

13 You say, "Food was made for the stomach, and the stomach for food". (This is true, though someday God will do away with both of them.) But you can't say that our bodies were made for sexual immorality. They were made for the Lord, and the Lord cares about our bodies' (1 Corinthians 6:12-13 NLT).

The Power of Waiting

The Bible, in the book of Ecclesiastes Chapter 3, tells us that there is a time and season for everything. Don't rush into marriage if you are dating; don't hurry to date if you are single. Pray about the timing. Be led by the

Holy Spirit. Age may be catching up to you, and you may even feel pressured to get married. But trust in the Lord's plans and timings for your life. He makes everything beautiful in His time. God's timing is perfect. There are no delays with Him.

'He has made everything beautiful in its time' (Ecclesiastes 3:11 NIV).

Wait for your Boaz. He was a rich and powerful man, yet he treated Ruth, a foreign woman in his land, with chivalry and respect. The story of Ruth and Boaz in the Bible is a story given to us by God as a model for courting and marriage. Take your time, wait for the right man, and I assure you it'll be worth it.

As women, we should run after God. Don't run after a man. The right man will eventually find his way to you when the time is right. God should be our priority and our first love. Desire to grow in your relationship with Him. We need to keep our eyes fixed on God. Don't make marriage the goal of your life. Don't live your entire life seeking out the man you want to marry. Instead, live your life seeking God and His kingdom. Don't seek Him only for what He can give you; rather, seek Him for who He is and what He has done for you. As you continue to love and serve Him, He will add these things to your bounty. He will give you the desires of your heart.

'But seek first his kingdom and his righteousness, and all these things will be given to you as well' (Matthew 6:33 NIV).

Life on earth is like a marathon. You train well and prepare yourself for it. You run with your eyes fixed on the finish line. Along the way, you may hit some obstacles that may slow you down; you may need to be re-energised. But you continue running at your pace until you find someone who can run along with you. He doesn't run faster or slower than you. He runs alongside you. He doesn't slow you down but he encourages and cheers you on. Then, you run together without looking back till the end to finish the marathon. This is a depiction of marriage.

Waiting shows that your desires don't govern your decisions. It is a gift of trust to your future husband. Wait to date if there is no one worth dating. Sometimes, we tend to jump ahead of ourselves out of boredom. Instead of choosing to date in your boredom, you can find a new hobby or polish an old skill. Never date out of boredom. Don't date because you feel lonely or incomplete either. It may make you feel good for a while, but the spiritual implications of it are greater in the formation of unwanted ungodly soul-ties.

Many times, we may need a period of waiting to get our heart and mind right with God. You may feel God leading you through a season of singleness. It is a wise decision to wait before you start dating. Wait till you're mature enough for a serious relationship. Persevere in prayer in your season of waiting. While you wait physically, you must grow spiritually. Use this time to focus on the Lord and grow in areas of your life that need maturing.

The Bible depicts the power of waiting through the story of Jacob and Rachel:

18 'Since Jacob was in love with Rachel, he told her father, "I'll work for you for seven years if you'll give me Rachel, your younger daughter, as my wife."

19 "Agreed!" Laban replied. "I'd rather give her to you than to anyone else. Stay and work with me".

20 So Jacob worked seven years to pay for Rachel. But his love for her was so strong that it seemed to him for only a few days.

21 Finally, the time came for him to marry her. "I have fulfiled my agreement," Jacob said to Laban. "Now give me my wife so I can sleep with her'" (Genesis 29:18-21 NLT).

23 'But that night, when it was dark, Laban took Leah to Jacob, and he slept with her....

25 But when Jacob woke up in the morning—it was Leah! "What have you done to me?" Jacob raged at Laban. "I worked seven years for Rachel! Why have you tricked me?"

26 "It's not our custom here to marry off a younger daughter ahead of the firstborn", Laban replied.

27 "But wait until the bridal week is over, then we'll give you Rachel, too—provided you promise to work another seven years for me'" (Genesis 29: 23, 25-27 NLT).

28 'So Jacob agreed to work seven more years. A week after Jacob had married Leah, Laban gave him Rachel, too. So Jacob slept with Rachel, too, and he loved her much more than Leah....

30 He then stayed and worked for Laban the additional seven years' (Genesis 29: 28, 30 NLT).

Jacob was in love with Rachel, but he had to wait a great deal of time before he could be with her. As he waited for Rachel, his love for her only grew stronger. Although he was angry when he was tricked by his father-in-law-to-be, he didn't storm off. Instead, he waited patiently for what was promised to him. He continued to work with integrity and to pursue his love for Rachel instead of giving up. Wait patiently for God to fulfil His promises in your life. He is a faithful God and always keeps His promises.

'God is not a man, so he does not lie. He is not human, so he does not change his mind. Has he ever spoken and failed to act? Has he ever promised and not carried it through?' (Numbers 23:19 NLT).

One of the greatest tests of true love is the ability to wait. Take the time to learn about your partner's desirable and undesirable traits. It will help you decide if you are willing to give yourself to selflessly loving and serving him for the rest of your lives together. Don't jump directly into marriage unless you are one hundred percent sure about him. Too often, couples marry in haste for the fear of losing their partner or the feelings of love. But it is better to be wise and wait rather than marry in a hurry and regret the decision later. Marriage is for life—there is no looking back once you're in it.

Love is a choice to continue serving him, despite his imperfections. Love looks out for the happiness and the good of the other person. It is not selfish. Love is willing to wait, if need be, to ensure that it is in the best interest of the other person. True love will stand the test of time. When you meet the right one, you'll know why it never worked out with anyone else and you will be thankful. Men like to pursue their partners. They like a good chase. They are always up for a challenge. Don't make it too easy for them. They enjoy the pursuit. So, allow him the satisfaction of pursuing you and enjoy being pursued.

Don't Isolate Yourself

God created us to be relational. We were never meant to live in isolation. We cannot live as islands to ourselves. Our lives are constantly affecting and are being affected by those around us. Hence, we need to maintain relationships with people other than our partner or spouse. Lean on other Christians who love you the most and have a record of telling you when you may be straying away from the will of God for your life. These are God-given people that support us, encourage us, and guide us on our journey in life. These are friendships for life; keep them close.

'Plans go wrong for lack of advice; many advisers bring success' *(Proverbs 15:22 NLT).*

If you really like someone and feel the leading of the Holy Spirit towards him, talk to someone above you. Talk to someone you trust and know will not gossip and spread rumours about you. Maybe you can speak to your parents about it or seek the counsel of your spiritual mentors or leaders. Parents and mentors have a way of intuition or a gut feeling about these things, especially about their children. They love us and have our best interests at heart. Ask them how they feel about your partner and the relationship? They might take some time to pray about it. God often uses spiritual authorities above us to confirm things He is already speaking to us. Sometimes, God also uses our unbelieving friends, especially close ones, to point out red flags in our partners. Don't dismiss their advice because they are unbelievers. Hear them out and take it to the Lord.

'My son, keep your father's command and do not forsake your mother's teaching. When you walk, they will guide you; when you sleep; they will watch over you; when you awake, they will speak to you' (Proverbs 6: 20, 22 NIV).

Dating can often isolate us from other relationships in our lives. Avoid keeping your relationship a secret. It can give the devil a foothold in your life. Secrets can open the doorways to different forms of temptation that will separate you from God and may even be dangerous for you. If you have to hide your relationship it is often because you think you're in the wrong. While you think you may be hiding it from everyone else, nothing is hidden from God. Resist the temptation to date in a corner by yourselves. Bring your relationship out in the open and seek godly counsel. Involve your partner in the existing relationships in your life, instead of isolating them. Spending more time around family and friends with your partner, grows the affection and communication in the relationship while dating.

Seek the advice of older married women in your local church, someone whose marriage you look up to. You may not always follow the advice they give but listen to what they have to say. They are wise and experienced in their years. They will be able to point out a potential red flag in your partner. Don't be triggered by what they say, instead take your time to pray about it. Is it something that can be overlooked or will it cause trouble in your marriage?

'These older women must train the younger women to love their husbands and their children, to live wisely and be pure, to work in their homes, to do good, and to be submissive to their husbands. Then they will not bring shame on the word of God' (Titus 2: 4-5 NLT).

We cannot walk this journey on this earth alone. Dating and marriage are not always a bed of roses. You need family, friends, and mentors who are not afraid to ask questions to protect you. They will persistently point you to Jesus, regardless of how it may make you feel.

Try New Things

The society that we live in today makes us believe that sex is the ultimate goal of life. Sex is on everyone's mind. Everyone appears to be curious about it. Some talk about it publicly, while others are hushed up and quiet behind closed doors. But everyone seems to be talking about it. It seems like you can't have a relationship without sex. The world today allows and, in fact, promotes pre-marital sex. According to the standards of the world, you first need to have sex. Everything else follows it. But that is not how God intended it to be. God designed sex to be shared between a man and a woman. It was made to be enjoyed in marriage. But since the fall of mankind, sin has perverted the hearts and minds of mankind. It has clouded our idea of right and wrong.

God's standards for us are much higher. It isn't because He is a killjoy. Rather, He knows that in obeying his commands and following His plans for us, we will be able to live an abundant and fulfilled life on this earth. He wants us to experience the contentment that comes from Him alone; the fulfilment of a commitment that cannot be obtained from the ways of the world.

Sex is not everything—there is so much more to life than just sex. Don't feel the need to sleep with each other. There are a number of other activities that you can do together. Find common ground in your relationship; find common interests. If your common interest is dance, try taking a few dance classes together. Or maybe you have a common interest in painting or cooking. You can perhaps paint or cook a meal together. Maybe the two of you enjoy being in nature. You can go trekking or even camping. Include a couple of friends. Or perhaps, it isn't a common interest but something that your partner really enjoys doing. It could be something you've never done before. You can try it out. Who knows, it might just become another one of your common interests.

Do activities that the two of you will enjoy together. It doesn't always have to be something that you excel in. Do it for the fun and joy of being together. Some things that you can do are try out a new restaurant, go for a walk in the country, go horseback riding, or maybe even have picnics in the car. There is no cap on the things you can do together as long as you aren't compromising on the laws set out in the Bible. Have 'clean fun' with each other. Enjoy each other's company while you're at it. You will realise that activities like these bring you closer to each other. They also provide opportunities to learn new things about your partner and get to know him better. You also create memories to last a lifetime. You can continue doing these activities even in marriage.

Finding new and fun things to do together is a good way to keep your relationship alive and exciting. It will help you break the monotony of life and the relationship. Couples often tend to get into a routine and can be easily bored. The key to an exciting relationship is in your hands. It is up to the two of you to work towards keeping your relationship alive. It is better to learn this early on in the relationship—it will reap good results for your marriage as well.

Facts vs. Fiction

Communication is the key to a healthy relationship. We must not assume things about the other person. It often starts with thoughts such as, 'I know what he's like,' 'I know why she...' 'I've seen this before', 'I know how this is going to end', 'I bet....'

We begin to form an opinion in our minds without confirming the facts of the situation. It is important to ask questions to distinguish the facts from fiction. We won't know what the other person is going through unless they make it known. Most of the time, things are not like how we thought them to be. It is also unfair to your partner to form an opinion about them based on assumptions or half-truths. Give them a chance to speak. Determine the whole truth.

Talk about your expectations in the relationship. What are you expecting from your partner in the relationship? Ask them what is expected of you. Talk about your likes and dislikes, your comfort zones, and your vision and future plans for the relationship. Don't leave God out of the picture. When you discuss these to determine the facts, you will get clarity on other aspects of the relationship—everything else becomes clear and easy to understand.

What are you expecting from the relationship? Do you see yourself marrying this man? How do they feel about the relationship? Are they serious about it? We cannot assume that our partner always wants the same thing as us. Make sure that the two of you are on the same page. What do you expect from them as a boyfriend or future spouse? Talk about how you expect to be treated. Don't assume that they just know and understand things. Be open and direct about what your expectations are. Be vocal about what you want and expect from them as a partner. It is similar to setting boundaries in your relationship.

When you do things together, don't assume they enjoy doing the same things as you. Talk about how you feel and listen to how they feel. Ask questions till you are sure you have understood what is communicated. Misinterpretation creates miscommunication and misunderstandings but the truth always wins.

Chapter 4:

Let Us Make Man in Our Image, After Our Likeness

'Then God said, "Let us make human beings in our image, to be like us. They will reign over the fish in the sea, the birds in the sky, the livestock, all the wild animals on the earth, and the small animals that scurry along the ground"'. (Genesis 1:26 NLT).

'Then the LORD God formed the man from the dust of the ground. He breathed the breath of life into the man's nostrils, and the man became a living person' (Genesis 2:7 NIV).

'So God created human beings in his own image. In the image of God he created them; male and female he created them' (Genesis 1:27 NLT).

God formed man out of the dust of the ground. He created a woman from the man. God created men and women differently with distinct roles and needs. It's what makes us so unique from each other. The world sometimes tells us that women can do what men can, and we can do it better. But God made us do what men can't do. God didn't make us different to compete and try to become like the opposite sex; rather, we were made to complement each other. We need to celebrate our differences and the way that God has uniquely created us. The Bible clearly lays out our roles and needs as men and women. Yes, Jesus levelled the spiritual playing field when He died on the cross for us. But we are still different in our needs and roles. How boring would it be if both men and women were exactly the same!

Understanding that men and women are wired differently is the key to a victorious relationship. Often, I've had people tell me that understanding the needs of the opposite sex is tougher than rocket science. They're probably the ones who never really made the effort to try and understand their partner. The Bible is our guide for everything including the basic needs of men and women, what can make us feel loved, and God's standard for us.

Many times, I hear couples say that they are poles apart or complete opposites. It's true, just as a man and a woman, you are different. That's how God made you. A woman's needs are very different from those of her husband. Although the primary need of both men and women is love, the way that each sex expresses and feels love also varies. This chapter explores the purpose of both the roles in a relationship and marriage.

'Husbands, love your wives, just as Christ also loved the church and gave Himself up for her' (Ephesians 5: 25 NIV).

'Each of you must also love his wife as he loves himself, and the wife must respect her husband' (Ephesians 5:33 NIV).

If love alone was sufficient, we wouldn't have so many marriages ending in divorce. The Bible tells us that while love is a necessity for a woman, men love in a different way. They love through respect. Men feel loved when they are respected. You can sometimes shower a man with all the love you have in your heart, but if you don't respect him, your love won't mean much to him. On the other hand, women love to be loved. Women need love. If the man tells his wife that he simply respects her, she will not feel loved enough.

Dr Emerson Eggerichs in his book, *Love and Respect*, brilliantly describes the needs of love and respect of women and men. He says, 'Wives are made to love, want to love and expect love. Men on the other hand are made to respect, want to respect and expect respect'.

This is why it is easy for a man to respect rather than to love, and for a woman to love rather than to respect. It's the way God has beautifully designed us to be different and unique from each other. It is also why He instructs us accordingly in the book of Ephesians Chapter 5.

Dr Emerson also talks about the crazy cycle—without love from him, she reacts without respect; and without respect from her, he reacts without love. If not kept under check, this crazy cycle can spin out of control. It can throw marriages off. Understanding this fundamental difference between men and women early on will help build a strong relationship. We need to understand how to love and respect according to God's standards.

What a Man Wants

Proverbs 31 describes a wife of noble character. It is God's standard for us as women. Be a woman of prayer who loves the Lord more than you love your man. It will set a strong foundation for loving him the right way. We need the grace of God and the help of the Holy Spirit to love and respect our partner in the way that he should be loved and respected.

Men also want a woman who is faithful and loyal. They look for domestic support in their partners—a good cook and someone who can keep the house in order. They want women who are secure in their identity. Since men are visually stimulated, they like women who are feminine and keep themselves well. They also want their wives to be good lovers and childbearing women. They often like to think of their partners as vixens. A Proverbs 31 woman would do the trick!

Notice how Ephesians Chapter 5 speaks about a woman 'respecting' her husband. As women, love comes more naturally to us. We find it easier to love. However, respect is something that we may struggle with, especially when it comes to respecting our partners. 'He doesn't deserve my respect!' is a comment that women often make. But the Bible calls us to show unconditional respect towards our partner and spouse.

Respect is every man's primary love language. It's one of his basic needs to feel loved. Even though he may have his identity in God, he still seeks validation from you as a partner. He cares about how you view him.

What you think about him matters to him. He wants you to be his biggest fan.

So, what can you do to make your man feel unconditionally loved (respected)? Here are a few ways in which you can love him in his love language of respect.

Verbally express to him that you value his efforts to work and provide for the family. When God created the world, he put the man to tend to and take care of it. He instilled deep in the hearts of man the desire to work and provide for the family. They are wired to strive to protect and provide for the family. It is why some men tend to feel a little insecure when their wives earn more than them. They think it is their responsibility to provide for the family. Many women complain that their husbands work too much. But often, the husband doesn't see any wrong in what he is doing. He thinks he is showing his love and commitment to the family by working long hours to provide for them. As women, we need to verbalise our respect for our partners in this area of provision. We need to value their effort to strive to provide for and keep the family healthy and happy.

Give him a listening ear, and listen intently especially, to his work stories. When you ask a man about his day, he is probably going to tell you about his work like that's the only thing he does. Sometimes, we tend to cut them off by telling them we don't want to hear any more about their work. But a man's work matters to him. It makes him feel respected when you show interest and care about his work.

Appreciate his commitment to protect the family. This is something that we often overlook or take for granted. God has designed them to shoulder the responsibility of taking care of the family.

A friend of mine once told me how she loved late-night drives with her husband—she enjoyed the thrill that came with it. But her husband would more than often refuse to take her out for her brief night adventures. And when they did go out, he was always cautious. Initially, she dismissed him as being silly. But she slowly came to realise the responsibility that he was shouldering to protect her from harm, and she now appreciates him for it. She says that while he may not always encourage her ideas of fun, he would certainly take a bullet for her. And that makes her feel safe when he's around.

Thank him for who is he and for the little things he does for you. Thank him for being your support and shoulder to lean on. Thank him for his godly counsel and insight on various issues. Praise his good decisions. Be graceful and slow to criticise him about the bad ones. In doing this, you will be able to love your man in the right way.

What a Woman Needs

The basic need of a woman is love. Women need affection. We want our partners to make us feel loved, even if it means going the extra mile. Women want to be cherished for who they are. They look for good communicators, men who will listen for feelings and emotions and not just words.

Women also often look to leadership in their man. According to the order that God has designed for a family unit, the husband is the head of the family just as Christ is the head of the church. A woman expects her husband to lead the family well as the spiritual head of the house. She wants a man who will uplift her in prayer in the hard times.

'For a husband is the head of his wife as Christ is the head of the church. He is the Saviour of his body, the church' (Ephesians 5:23 NLT).

Women also want to feel safe around their partner or spouse. They look for financial, emotional, and spiritual security in their man. A woman wants a man who is understanding. Someone who will understand her needs, especially when she is physically or emotionally drained. In such times, she wants her man to step up and help around the house. Women want a man who is committed to serving his family. They want a good father for their children, someone who will help them bring up the children in the ways of the Lord.

Women also enjoy a good pursuit. They like their men to pursue them, not only in the years of courtship or dating but also in marriage. Couples tend to stop dating each other once they are married. However, dating each other in marriage will give you a break from the busyness and routine of life. It will also give you quality time with each other and keep the relationship alive.

Women want to be loved unconditionally. But unless your man first understands the love of Christ, he may struggle with loving you unconditionally. Pray for your man and ask God to continue to pour His love into his heart every day.

The Future

Before you discuss the future with your partner, ask yourself these questions. Do you see a future with this person? Do you see him as the father of your children? Do you want to spend the rest of your life with him and grow old together? If the answer to these questions is a big yes, you can move on to discussing your future with this man.

It's important to think of your future with your partner. Talk about when you want to get married. Why do you want to get married? Do you want children? How many children do you want? These may seem like intimidating questions to discuss, but they are important in knowing where the two of you stand in your relationship. These are questions that will also need to be answered prayerfully.

Do you understand the role of a husband? Will you be able to submit to his leadership? Are you ready for a lifetime of commitment? If these questions scare you, take some time to seek the Lord and discern if you are ready to get married. It is important that you mentally prepare yourself for marriage. It is not a getaway or escape from your current situation rather, marriage is a huge responsibility and you need to be prepared for it.

Often couples that fall out of marriage unions say that they need to focus on their personal growth and individual careers. This can well be an excuse to end the marriage amicably after the usefulness of the 'partnership' has been served. However, Christ calls us to a much higher standard. Even if you want to pursue individual things, it can be done with the full support of your spouse. Fallouts in Christian marriages may happen when the couple doesn't share a common vision in Christ for their marriage.

An important aspect of your future together that is often overlooked, is your ministry as a couple. How will the two of you be serving together in your local church? What ministry is God calling you to as a couple? As a couple, the most important factor in your relationship is knowing how you will serve God together. What is the purpose of your union? Good Christian marriages are a blessing to the community. Prayerfully seek the Lord about the vision or mission for your marriage. It is also wise to seek the counsel of your mentors and leaders, as they will be able to guide you and point you in the right direction. The mission of your marriage is often what will keep the two of you pursuing the Lord together. Have a clear vision for your marriage. Surrender your mission into the Lord and trust the leading and direction of the Holy Spirit to fulfil it. You may have different missions for different seasons in your marriage, although the vision might stay the same.

Make a commitment to build the foundation of your marriage on Jesus so that, no matter what comes against you, your union will continue to stay strong in the Lord.

'Though one may be overpowered, two can defend themselves. A cord of three strands is not quickly broken' (Ecclesiastes 4:12 NIV).

Never leave God out of the equation, especially when planning your future together. He needs to be at the centre of your lives and decisions. Everything you do in your marriage in the future needs to be centred on Christ. It will bring glory to His name. As a Christian, your relationship or marriage should be a reflection of Christ's love. In everything you do, your life should be an example and a light to the darkness in the world outside.

'Let your light shine before others, that they may see your deeds and glorify your Father in heaven' (Matthew 5:16 NIV).

The Purpose of Marriage

The Bible in the book of Genesis Chapter 2 talks about God's original plan for marriage. It describes the marriage union between a man and woman as becoming one in the flesh. The Bible considers the marriage union as sacred. God is the one who joins a man and woman together in holy matrimony. The Bible instructs us that no one is to break or separate what God has joined together.

'Therefore, a man shall leave his father and his mother and hold fast to his wife, and they shall become in flesh' (Genesis 2:24 ESV).

'And the two will become one flesh. So they no longer two, but one flesh. Therefore, what God has joined together, let no one separate' (Mark 10:8-9 NIV).

Marriage is not rooted in our feelings alone as feelings are here today and gone tomorrow. But marriage is a covenant. It is about keeping a promise, with God as the witness.

"You cry out, "Why doesn't the LORD accept my worship?" I'll tell you why! Because the LORD witnessed the vows you and your wife made when you were young' (Malachi 2:14 NLT).

Marriage is more about Jesus than it is us. The Apostle Paul in the book of Ephesians talks about the purpose of marriage. He uses marriage to illustrate the relationship that Christ shares with the church. Marriage is designed upon the union of God with His people.

'As the scriptures say, "A man leaves his father and mother and is joined to his wife, and the two are united into one". This is a great mystery, but it is an illustration of the way Christ and the church are one' (Ephesians 5:31-32 NLT).

Marriage is about two people making a covenant to love each other unconditionally, through every high and low, in sickness and health for the rest of their lives. It symbolises Christ's covenant relationship with the church. It reflects Christ's sacrificial, unconditional, and unending love for the church, his bride. The Bible talks about an 'agape' love that Christ has for the church. Agape love is divine love; it is unconditional love. It doesn't depend on the merits or demerits of the recipient. It depends on the nature of the giver. Agape love expects nothing in return; it is a hundred percent giving love. It is a love that looks out for the good of the other person at a personal expense. When we love with an agape love, our marriage becomes a beautiful picture of the gospel of grace. This is God's purpose for us in marriage. It is the standard that he has set for us. It is why any other version of marriage is damaging as it distorts the picture that God designed for marriage. However, we will never be able to reach God's standard for our marriage in our own strength. We need the help of the Holy Spirit to enjoy the fullness of marriage as God intended it to be.

Marriage was given to us by God to enjoy and display the gospel. It was given so that through godly marriages, the name of the Lord will be glorified. We are called to honour God through our marriage by first submitting to His laws and then to the laws of the land. We acknowledge the purpose of marriage in our lives by publicly declaring our love and commitment to each other through our marriage vows.

Christ calls us to be kind, selfless, and forgiving towards our spouses. We are called to an unending love and mutual submission to each other in Christ. In doing so, we will present the gospel to the world and fulfil the purpose for which marriage was created.

One of the most important decisions you will make is deciding who you will marry. However, the Apostle Paul tells us that marriage is not for everyone. God may call you to a life of singleness in serving Him. You don't find your purpose through marriage; you find your purpose in God. Paul also says that marriage brings many troubles—this is inevitable. Paul exhorts us to live our lives devoted to the Lord, whether through marriage or singleness. Marriage should not be a distraction from serving the Lord.

'But those who marry will face many troubles in this life. I am saying this for your own good, not to restrict you, but that you may live in a right way in undivided devotion to the Lord' (1 Corinthians 7:28, 35 NLT).

While no marriage is perfect, work towards making a good marriage into a glimpse of heaven on earth. Marriage is hard work, but with the Holy Spirit as our helper, we can have fun and spirit-filled marriages that will bring glory to God and present the gospel to the world.

Chapter 5:

Let There Be Light

'But everything exposed by the light becomes visible—and everything that is illuminated becomes a light' (Ephesians 5:13 NIV).

Society teaches men to be strong. They are often belittled when they show emotion and are judged by the figure that they make. Society puts undue pressure on men to hold it together in every situation. But it is not how God made them. This chapter discusses men as God intended them to be. It also aims to reveal some of the secrets and struggles within a man's heart.

The Secrets of Men Made Simple

Maybe you've noticed your man get uncomfortable when you talk about his salary at work. Or perhaps, he is awkward when faced with situations that involve a display of emotions, especially tears. Most men are always trying to act stronger than they are because of what society teaches them. It almost seems like they are not allowed to feel and express emotions, especially those of pain, hurt, or sorrow. However, men feel every emotion that women do. They are often ashamed of it.

They don't want you to know that they emote for the fear of not being good enough in your eyes. So, they often try to suppress how they really feel.

However, emotions are a way of releasing the feelings within us. Emotions help us deal with situations in life on earth. It's what makes us, us. When God created man in His image, He created them as emotional beings. Yes, God is powerful and mighty, but He is also full of emotion. The Scriptures show God displaying a wide range of emotions. He was sorry and grieved when man sinned against Him. God was angry when His people made idols for themselves and worshipped other gods. God is also abounding in love and mercy. The Bible tells us that He also delights in the praises of His people. He is also compassionate towards His people. In the New Testament, the Bible tells us that Jesus wept when Lazarus died.

'Then God said, "Let us make mankind in our image, in our likeness"' Genesis 1:26 NIV).

'So the LORD was sorry he has ever made them and put them on the earth. It broke his heart' (Genesis 6:6 NLT).

'Remember and never forget how angry you made the LORD your God out in the wilderness. From the day you left Egypt until now, you have been constantly rebelling against him' (Deuteronomy 9:7 NLT).

'And he passed in front of Moses, proclaiming, "The LORD, the LORD, the compassionate and gracious God, slow to anger, abounding in love and faithfulness"' (Exodus 34:6 NIV).

Our emotions and feelings are normal and natural—they come from God. But sometimes, we can be misled by our emotions. They can cause us to sin against God. On the other hand, God's emotions are always righteous and stem from a genuine and true love for His people.

More than often, it's not that men don't want to show emotion. Rather, they struggle to show it as emotions have always been perceived as for the weak. They won't want you to think they are weaklings. However, men tend to show the emotion of anger very well. The world has a false notion that anger and violence are a display of power and somehow make you seem stronger. It is also why so many men with insecurities in their lives often resort to anger and abuse towards their wives.

I believe that strong and mature Christian men are those that have allowed God to work in their lives. They have allowed God to heal their hearts and they understand how God designed them to be. They know and believe that they are fearfully and wonderfully made in the image of the living God. And they are not afraid to show emotion even if it means being mocked for it. As women, we need to be supportive of our partners and not ridicule them for showing emotion. In fact, I assure you that a man who is not afraid to express his emotions will also be able to love you better.

My friend, Kevin, now a leader in his local church, grew up with an unbelieving and abusive dad. His dad would often physically abuse his mother for being a believer in

Christ. As the older son, Kevin would always intervene to try and protect his mum. He's seen his mum cry every time she was abused, and he says that it used to break his heart. Seeing his mum cry would make him cry too, and his dad often mocked him for it. But as a little boy, he was trying to be strong.

Once, after a terrible fight between his parents, he was done crying. He was done being 'weak'. So, he made a vow to never cry again. And he stuck by it. He didn't shed a tear for the next 18 years of his life, even if he wanted to. Yes, he did feel pain and hurt but took to other self-harming ways to release his feelings.

About a year into marriage, when he was attending a healing and deliverance conference with his wife, God ministered to his heart. The Holy Spirit reminded him of the vow he had made and brought certain events from his childhood to remembrance. With the help of his mentor, Kevin repented and broke the vow he had made. He was almost immediately able to release the pain and hurt he had been holding on to for so long, especially towards his dad. He was able to release forgiveness towards him. He says he remembers weeping like a child and it was the best thing he had felt in a long time. Kevin's life is just one such powerful testimony of the goodness and mercy of God.

Another thing that most men don't want to talk about is their salary. This often upsets women. They often argue that there should be no secrets in marriage. But as women, we need to understand a man's heart.

When it comes to a man, he wants to keep his woman as happy as can be. They want to give their wives and children the best of everything. It is often how they validate themselves and measure their love for their family. Most men firmly believe that it is their job to provide for the family, come what may. So, they find it irrelevant to discuss how much they make. They want you to trust them to work hard to provide for you and the family. Sometimes, some men may feel like they aren't making enough to give you a fulfiling life. Society often portrays beautiful women as going after wealthy men. It is important for you to assure your husband that their worth does not depend on their salary, but on the value that God places on them. You need to affirm that you love them not for the money they make but for who they are. You need to assure them that you will stick by them for better or worse. Appreciate and respect their effort to work hard and provide for the family. As you begin to assure him and respect him, he will eventually open up to you about his life, including his finances. Assure him that you will be a support to him in any way that you can if things ever get tough. As he leans on your trust and encouragement, he will push himself to do better and be a better spouse to you.

Discussing Family Roles and Relationships

At the beginning of creation, God and man were in a relationship with each other. The man was complete in God. God made man and told him to tend to the earth and take care of it. But then God said that it was not good for man to be 'alone'. So He decided to make a suitable helper for him. The man wasn't 'lonely'. God didn't create a woman to make men feel less lonely. He created her to be a suitable helper for him to help him tend to the garden. Man and woman, husband and wife were supposed to be hand-in-glove. They were supposed to be the dream team. But the fall of mankind has distorted God's design for the family unit. It has clouded the relationship between man and wife.

'The LORD God said, "It is not good for the man to be alone. I will make a helper suitable for him". Then the LORD God made a woman from the rib he had taken out of the man, and he brought her to the man' (Genesis 2:18, 22 NIV).

'To the woman he said, "Your desire will be for your husband, and he will rule over you"' (Genesis 3:16).

Notice how the Bible uses the word *alone* and not *lonely*. Imagine you're travelling on the subway. There's no one else on the coach but you. You're alone, but you don't necessarily have to be lonely. You know you have a family back home. You might even call up a friend to keep you company as you travel alone. On the other hand, you could be in a room full of people and connect to no one. You may have friends and family and feel like no one understands and relates to you. Chances are that you are lonely. God doesn't want you to marry because you feel lonely. He has designed marriage to be a beautiful companionship between man and woman, where you support each other as you are first complete in God.

God designed the governmental order for marriage. He calls husbands to exercise a role of self-sacrificial leadership or headship over the family. Wives are called to godly submission towards their husbands. As women, we have to let our husbands lead us. Often, when men fail to lead the family, the wife is forced to step up. But this bends the governmental order that God designed for the family unit.

22 'Wives, submit yourselves to your own husbands as you do to the Lord.

23 For the husband is the head of the wife as Christ is the head of the church, his body, of which he is the Saviour.

24 Now as the church submits to Christ, so wives should submit to their husbands in everything.

25 Husbands, love your wives, just as Christ loved the church and gave himself up for her' (Ephesians 5:22-25 NIV).

Men were made to be spiritual leaders and providers in the house. Women are not made to handle the kind of pressure that comes with providing for the family. However, in certain circumstances, when women are forced to step up, God does give them the grace to handle the situations. Some women work and earn more than their partners or husbands. There's nothing wrong with it, as long as we still allow our husbands to lead the family. Assure him that you still need his love and support. Discuss practical ways how you will continue to be led by him. Let pride never come in the way of a fruitful and blessed marriage.

As women, we are called to submit to our husbands. It is not a dominating or forceful submission. We need to model Christ and his love for the church. Christ loves us— His church—yet He does not force us to follow Him. He gave His life for us in fully knowing that we might reject him. Still, He loves us unconditionally. Our submission to Christ is an act of obedience. It also is a response to His sacrificial love for us as the Holy Spirit has revealed it to us. It is the same in marriage. Wives are called to unconditional respect towards their husbands, and husbands are called to unconditional love towards their wives.

26 'For you are all children of God through faith in Christ Jesus.

27 And all who have been united with Christ in baptism have put on Christ, like putting on new clothes.

28 There is no longer Jew or Gentile, slave or free, male or female. For you are all one in Christ Jesus' (Galatians 3:26-28 NLT).

Men and women are equal but different. Men and women are equal in spiritual aspects. But we are different in our physical, psychological, and temperamental make-up. We need to recognise these differences that God has given us. These differences give rise to different roles. It is about the responsibility that God has bestowed on us as men and women. God has designed separate roles for men and women in the context of marriage and governmental order in the house.

It's similar to the working of the army. While one person is in command, every soldier has to work together as a team. The general needs his troops to fight the war, just as much as they need him to lead them. Chaos would ensue if everyone had the same roles to play in the army. The soldiers, together with the able leading of their commander, can fight the battle and emerge victoriously.

We need to stop competing with the opposite sex. Don't compete against your husband. Instead, complement him in a way that completes your union. Learn to work as a team. The husband and wife have to be a loving team modelled after the Triune God. There must be security and order for anything to flourish in the long run, especially, in a family where children are involved. Work as a team with a vision and purpose for growth and development beyond each other.

Discuss family relationships with your partner. Does he keep in touch with his parents? Does he honour and respect them? What about his siblings? Does he share a good relationship with them? There could be unresolved issues in his heart. Encourage him to deal with them before he gets into marriage. Sanctification is a life-long process and marriage should help us become more like Jesus.

How to Talk about Past Relationships

It is important to discuss past relationships with your partner to prevent awkward situations in the future. Often, men might not want you to know how many sexual partners they have had in the past. While it may be a difficult topic to discuss, we need to remember in God's eyes sin is sin. There is no greater and lesser sin. Remember that no one is perfect. We all falter and fail.

It is the grace and mercy of God that carries us through. If we have asked God to forgive us from our past ways, He has washed us clean. He has taken away the guilt and shame.

Has he truly repented from his ways? Has there been a visible change in his life since then? Are there still any sinful patterns that could cause trouble for your marriage in the future? You need to know and understand what he will be carrying into the relationship with you. Has he been married before? Why did the previous marriage or relationship fall out? Does he have any kids from his previous relationships? If yes, how are you going to handle the situation? Are you up for a relationship like that?

This is often a sensitive topic to discuss for most men. Be empathetic and understanding. Ask God for grace to look at them as He sees them—not as damaged goods but as the finished product. Listen to them without judging them. Address these questions to encourage the feeling of complete nakedness in the relationship. Bring it all out in the open and lay it out on the table no matter what the other person thinks.

This sense of openness allows you to fully understand and know what you are getting into. It brings in a feeling of confidence in knowing that neither of you is putting up a front. So, you don't have to pretend to be someone you're not. You can be around each other knowing that the other person fully accepts you for who you are despite everything that has happened in your life. It brings in a feeling of trust and security in the relationship. It is love in its truest and purest form. It allows you to be truly naked with the other person—

naked with your soul and not just physical nakedness. It is how God designed the marriage union to be—without shame. Complete openness with each other will create a deeper and more intimate bond between the two of you. It models Christ's love and acceptance for us while we were still sinners:

'Now the man and his wife were both naked, but they felt no shame' (Genesis 2:25 NLT).

Another aspect to consider and discuss is financial burdens. Are there any financial issues that he is struggling with? Is there anything that could add unnecessary and unwanted financial stress in the future? Does he struggle with handling money? While no man is perfect, it is worth knowing what you're getting into rather than regretting your decision to marry years down the line.

These sensitive discussions are often harder for the person on the receiving end. Remember, however, that God didn't think twice about loving us when we were sinners. Jesus still chose to die for us. God doesn't think twice when we go to Him every time we fall and ask for forgiveness. Be merciful just as you would expect to be shown mercy.

'God blesses those who are merciful, for they will be shown mercy' (Matthew 5:7 NLT).

Who Are His Mentors?

We need to have someone in our lives who we can be accountable to, especially if we've struggled with hidden sin in the past. These could be spiritual mentors, leaders, or close Christian friends or family. They are people who will point out blind spots in your life and help you keep your life on track with Jesus. They cry with you and uphold you in prayer in the tough times. They probably know everything there is to your life.

Does your partner have a mentor? Who is he? Who are his role models? Is he accountable to anyone? Many may argue that Jesus is our best role model and the Holy Spirit is the best mentor we can have. While absolutely true, we need to be accountable to godly people who we can trust because they help keep our lives in check. You can tell a lot about a person based on who their role model is. People often want to imitate and become like their role models.

Does he have problems with submitting to authority? Is he submissive to his church leaders? God places godly authority over our lives to encourage and edify us. We need to honour and respect their authority over our lives. We may not agree with them about everything, but we must still choose to respect them.

'Confess your sins to each other and pray for each other so that you may be healed. The earnest prayer of a righteous person has great power and produces wonderful results' (James 5:16 NLT).

'Remember your leaders who taught you the word of God. Think of all the good that has come from their lives, and follow the example of their faith' (Hebrews 13:17 NLT).

'Brother and sister, if someone is caught in a sin, you who live by the Spirit should restore that person gently. But watch yourselves, or you also may be tempted. Carry each other's burdens, and in this way you will fulfil the law of Christ' (Galatians 6:1-2 NIV).

Chapter 6:

Get to Know Your Coach

Congratulations on completing the book. As you've come this far, I trust that the Holy Spirit will lead you in making the right decisions. I pray that you will be led and guided in His direction for your life. I believe that God will honour you for seeking His will and plans for your life. He will give you the desires of your heart.

I am aware that some of you reading this are not Born-Again Christian believers.

Have you ever made Jesus the Lord and Saviour of your life?

If not, pray this prayer and start a new life in Christ.

Dear God,

I come to You in the Name of Jesus. I admit that I am not right with You, and I want to be right with You. I ask You to forgive me of all my sins. The Bible says if I confess with my mouth that 'Jesus is Lord,' and believe in my heart that God raised Him from the dead, I will be saved (Rom. 10:9). I believe with my heart and I confess with my mouth that Jesus is the Lord and Saviour of my life. Thank You for saving me!

In Jesus' name I pray. Amen.

For a personal tailor made one to one coaching and group sessions please send an email to: venicialloyd@gmail.com

Please write a review on Amazon sharing your experience.

Conclusion

God has made us relational. We were created to be in a relationship with God and each other. As women, we often struggle with making the right choices about the one we want to marry. But we have a God who leads and guides us every step of the way.

Be specific about what you desire in your spouse. Make a list of things and pray about them every day till you see it come to pass in your life. Choose a Christian man. Do not enter into marriage with your blindfold of love in your eyes. Look for the red flags and seek wisdom and discernment from the Holy Spirit. Set spiritual, physical, relational, and emotional boundaries to keep you from falling into temptation and dishonouring the name of the Lord. Be clear about your intention for marriage. Deal with any baggage you could be carrying before you start dating. Know that you are complete in God. You are accepted and loved by Him. Live out the standard that God has set for you in Proverbs 31 as a woman.

Love is not just a feeling; it is a decision and a choice that we must make every day. We love out of the love that we have received in our hearts from God. The Bible lays out God's standard of love for us in 1 Corinthians Chapter 13. The more love we receive from God, the more we will want to give it—loved people love others. Communication is the key to a healthy relationship. Don't assume things about your partner.

Gently express your thoughts, feelings, and opinions. Communication is a two-way line—take time to listen to your partner. Understand your partner's love language.

Take your time in getting to know your partner. Don't rush into what can become an ungodly soul-tie. Enjoy a healthy friendship without labelling it. Don't get carried away by your feelings for your partner. Trust God and not your feelings. Don't isolate yourself from existing relationships in your life. Try new activities together. Save the sex for marriage as God designed it to be. While in your season of singleness and waiting, grow in your relationship with God. Run after God and the right man will eventually find his way to you.

The primary need of a man is respect and of a woman is love. Learn to unconditionally respect your man. Talk about the future. Pray about your vision and ministry as a couple. Let your marriage display the gospel of grace.

God made men and women unique. We are equal but different in our roles. We are called to complement and not compete with each other. Men often struggle with expressing emotions. They find it hard to discuss their salary and past relationships. Be empathetic and understanding. Know his mentors and role models. Be accountable to godly authority above you.

In doing this, by the grace of God and the help of the Holy Spirit, you will fulfil God's calling for you in your singleness and marriage and live to glorify His Name.

References

Chapman, G. D., & Summers, A. (2010). *The five love languages: How to express heartfelt commitment to your mate*. Lifeway Press.

Eggerichs, E. (2005). *Love & respect workbook*. Integrity Publishers, Colorado Springs, Colo.

FastStats—Marriage and divorce. (2019). Centers for Disease Control and Prevention. https://www.cdc.gov/nchs/fastats/marriage-divorce.htm

Lewis, C. S. (1952). *Mere Christianity: Comprising the case for Christianity, Christian behaviour, and beyond personality*. Harpercollins.

Six in ten single women have already planned aspects of their wedding. (2014, February 25). Mail Online. https://www.dailymail.co.uk/femail/article-2567408/Bridezilla-Britain-Six-ten-SINGLE-women-planned-wedding-including-dress-flowers-bridesmaids.html

www.ingramcontent.com/pod-product-compliance
Lightning Source LLC
Chambersburg PA
CBHW071008120726
47910CB00004B/1431